W9-CMP-655

COYOTE AND
QUARTER-MOON

Coyote and Quarter-Moon

WESTERN STORIES

Bill Pronzini

FIVE STAR

An imprint of Thomson Gale, a part of The Thomson Corporation

THOMSON

GALE

Detroit • New York • San Francisco • New Haven, Conn. • Waterville, Maine • London

THOMSON

™

GALE

LIBRARY OF CONGRESS CATALOGING-IN-PUBLICATION DATA

Pronzini, Bill.
    Coyote and quarter-moon : western stories / by Bill Pronzini. — 1st ed.
      p. cm.
    "A Five Star western"—T.p. verso.
    ISBN 1-59414-405-2 (alk. paper)
    1. Western stories. I. Title.
PS3566.R67C68 2006
813'.54—dc22   2006021487

U.S. Hardcover:
ISBN 13: 978-1-59414-405-9
ISBN 10: 1-59414-405-2

First Edition. First Printing: November 2006.

Published in 2006 in conjunction with Golden West Literary Agency.

Printed in the United States of America on permanent paper
10 9 8 7 6 5 4 3 2 1

CONTENTS

DEVIL'S BREW

There were few more undesirable places for a detective and temperance man to be plying his trade, Quincannon reflected sourly, not for the first time in the past week, than the bowels of a blasted brewery.

The fine, rich perfume of malt, hops, yeast, and brewing and fermenting beer permeated every nook and cranny of the two-story, block-square brick building that housed Golden Gate Steam Beer. Whenever he prowled its multitude of rooms and passages, he was enveloped in a pungent miasma that tightened and dried his throat, created a thirst that plain water couldn't quite slake. In his drinking days he had been mightily fond of the type of lager, invented during the Gold Rush and unique to San Francisco, known as steam beer. John Wieland's Philadelphia Brewery, the National Brewery, and others operating in the city in this year of 1896 specialized in porter and pilsner; if one of their owners had sought his services, he would not be suffering such pangs as this place instilled in him. But it had been Golden Gate's James Carreaux who had come calling, and the fee plus bonus he'd offered for an investigation into the bizarre death of his head brewmaster was a sum no Scot in his right mind could afford to turn down.

In the five years since Quincannon had taken the pledge, he had seldom been even mildly tempted to return to his bibulous ways. Even on those occasions when he visited his old watering hole, Hoolihan's Saloon, to spend an evening with cronies or clients, he hadn't once considered imbibing anything stronger than his usual mug of clam juice. But after one full week of undercover work in the Golden Gate's rarified atmosphere, his craving for a tankard of San Francisco's best lager had grown to the barely manageable level. Another week here and he might well be seduced.

Well, it was a moot point. He wouldn't be here in the guise of a city sanitation inspector for a second week, or even for one more day. There was no longer any doubt that Otto Ackermann's death had been a deliberate homicide, not the freak accident the authorities had ruled it to be. He knew who had manufactured what Carreaux referred to as a "devil's brew" by coshing Ackermann and pitching him into a vat of fermenting beer to drown, and he was tolerably certain he knew the reason behind the deed. All that was needed now was additional proof.

Instead of entering the brewery with the arriving employees, as he had on previous mornings, Quincannon loitered outside the main entrance. The cold, fog-laden March wind was much preferable to the brewery perfume. He smoked his pipe, feigning interest in the big dray wagons laden with both full and empty kegs that passed by on Fremont Street.

Caleb Lansing, the assistant brewmaster, was among the last to arrive, heavily bundled in cap, bandanna, and peacoat. He barely glanced at Quincannon as he passed and entered the building. Quincannon essayed a small, satisfied smile around the stem of his briar. Lansing had no idea that he was about to be yaffled for his crime; if he had, he would have taken it on the lammas by now.

When Quincannon finished his pipe, he strolled briskly to Market Street, where he boarded a westbound streetcar. He rode it as far as Duboce, walked the two blocks south to Fourteenth Street—a workingman's neighborhood of beer halls, oyster dealers, Chinese laundries, grocers, and other small merchants.

The front door of the boarding house where Lansing hung his hat was unlocked; he sauntered in as if he belonged there, climbed creaking stairs to the second floor. The hallway there was deserted. He paused before the door bearing a pot-metal numeral **8** and tested the latch. Locked, of course. Not that this presented much of a problem. Quincannon had developed certain skills during his years with the United States Secret Service and subsequent time as a private investigator, some of which rivaled those of the most accomplished yeggs and cracksmen. The set of burglar tools he had liberated from a scruff named Wandering Ned several years ago gave him swift access to Lansing's two small rooms.

Both sitting room and bedroom were cluttered with personal items, as well as several bottles of rye whiskey, but no steam beer. Lansing evidently had little taste for what he helped brew. In the fireplace grate Quincannon found a partially charred note penned in a sprawling backhand. Much of its content was unburned and legible, including an injunction from the writer to Lansing to destroy it after reading. Also present and damning was the writer's signature: **X.J.** Very few men in San Francisco could lay claim to those initials. The only one Quincannon knew of was Xavier Jameson, the head brewmaster at one of Golden Gate's rivals, West Coast Steam Beer.

His second discovery took longer, but was equally rewarding. In a small strongbox cleverly concealed behind a loose board in the bedroom closet he found $2,000 in greenbacks and a handful of gold double eagles. As much as he enjoyed the look and feel of spendable currency, he hesitated only a few seconds before returning the money to the strongbox, and the strongbox to its hiding place.

Criminals—*faugh!* The lot of them were arrogant and careless dolts. Lansing's failure to burn the note completely and his hiding of the pay-off money here in his rooms, coupled with the testimony of the witness who had seen him entering the brewery late on the night of Ackermann's death, his denial of the fact, and a slip he'd made that revealed his dealings with Xavier Jameson and West Star Steam Beer, were more than sufficient evidence to hang him.

Quincannon whistled an old temperance tune—"The Brewers' Big Horses Can't Run Over Me"—as he left the boarding house. Naught was left but to confront Lansing, urge a confession out of him through one means or another, and hand him over to those inept, blue-coated denizens of the Hall of Justice who had the audacity to call themselves San Francisco's finest. Then he could return to the relative peace and clean air of the offices of Carpenter and Quincannon, Professional Detective Services, where his only temptation—one he yearned to succumb to—was the charms of his partner and unrequited love, Sabina Carpenter.

Golden Gate's business offices were clustered at the east end of the second floor, all of them small and cramped except for James Carreaux's. This was Quincannon's first stop upon his return, but Caleb Lansing was not in his office. Waiting there for the assistant brewmaster was not an option; he was anything but a patient man when he was about to yaffle a miscreant. He went down the hall to the nearest occupied office, that of the company bookkeeper, Adam Corby, and poked his head inside.

"Would you know where I can find Lansing, Mister Corby?"

Corby, a bantam of a man in striped galluses and rough twill trousers, paused in his writing in an open ledger book. "Lansing? Why, no, I don't."

"When did you see him last?"

10

"Just after I arrived this morning. Have you tried the brew house?"

"My next stop."

The brew house was at the opposite end of the building. Lansing was nowhere to be found in the rooms containing the malt storage tanks and mash tun. Jacob Drew, the mash boss, a red-haired, red-bearded giant, reported that he'd seen Lansing in the fermenting room a few minutes earlier.

"What d'ye want with him, mister?" Drew asked. "Something to do with your inspection?"

"No. Another matter entirely."

"The lad's a weak stick, but he's done competent work since poor Ackermann's accident."

"That he has," Quincannon said. "Though not in the brewer's art."

He left Drew looking puzzled and followed a sinuous maze of piping to the fermenting room, a cavernous space filled with gas-fired cookers and cedar-wood fermenting tanks some nine feet in height and circumference. Two of the cookers contained bubbling wort—an oatmeal-like mixture of water, mashed barley, and soluble starch turned into fermentable sugar during the mashing process. After the wort was hopped and brewed, it would be filtered and fermented to produce steam beer—a term that had nothing to do with the use of actual steam. The lager was made with bottom-fermenting yeast at 60-70 degrees Fahrenheit, rather than the much lower temperatures necessary for true lager fermentation, because the city's winters were never cold enough to reach the freezing point. Additional keg fermentation resulted in a blast of foam and the loud hiss of escaping carbon dioxide when the kegs were tapped, a sound not unlike the release of a steam boiler's relief valve.

The heady aroma was strongest here. Once again Quincannon's nostrils began to quiver, his mouth and throat to feel like the inside of a corroded drainpipe. He wished, ruefully, that a man could be fitted with a relief valve as easily as a boiler, to ease pressure build-up inside his head.

On the catwalk above the cookers, Caleb Lansing stood supervising the adding of dried hops to the cooking wort. Workmen with long-handled wooden paddles stirred the mixture, while others skimmed off the dark, lumpy scum called krausen, a mixture of hop-resin, yeast, and impurities that rose to the surface. The slab floor, supported by heavy steel girders, was slick with globs of foam that a hose man sluiced at intervals into the drains.

Quincannon hastened to climb the stairs. From the catwalk, the cooking wort and interiors of the fermenting vats were visible. An unappetizing view, to be sure. The vat in which Ackermann had died had been cleaned and was no longer in use, but Quincannon's imagination was sufficient to conjure up the scene that had confronted the workmen the morning after.

Lansing was a rumpled, obsequious sort in his middle years, given to smoking odiferous long nines; cigar ash littered his loose-hanging vest and shirt front. He had just finished consulting a turnip watch when he spied Quincannon. Sudden anxious tension pulled his vulpine features out of shape. The look of a guilty man, by grab; Quincannon had seen it often enough to know it well.

Lansing swung away from the low railing, came forward as he approached, and sought to push past him. Quincannon blocked his way. "I'll have a word with you, Lansing."

"Not now you won't. Can't you see I'm busy?"

"My business with you won't wait."

"What business?"

"Otto Ackermann. Xavier Jameson. And the West Star Brewing Company."

Fright shone in the assistant brewmaster's narrow face. "I

don't know what you're talking about."

"The game's up, Lansing. I know the whole lay."

Lansing said—"Damned fly cop!"—under his breath and shoved past him. He would have run then if Quincannon hadn't grabbed the trailing flap of his vest and yanked him around.

"No trouble now, or you'll. . . ."

The blasted scoundrel was quick as a cat, not with his hands but with his feet. The toe of his heavy work shoe *thudded* painfully into Quincannon's shin, sent him staggering backward against the railing. Lansing fled to the stairs, clattered down them as Quincannon, growling an oath, regained his balance and hobbled in pursuit.

"Stop him!" he shouted at the workers below. "Stop that man!"

"No, no, don't let him catch me!" Lansing cried in return. "He's an assassin . . . he's trying to kill me!"

The workers stood in clustered confusion, looking from one to the other of the running men. Lansing threaded through them, vaulted an intestinal coiling of pipes, and disappeared behind one of the vats. Quincannon might have snagged him before he escaped from the fermenting room if a mustached workman hadn't stepped into his path, saying: "Here, what's the idea of . . . ?" Quincannon bowled him over, but in doing so his foot slipped on the wet floor and he went skidding headfirst into a snake-like tangle of hose. By the time he disengaged himself and regained his feet, fought off clutching hands, and went ahead in a limping rush, Lansing was nowhere to be seen.

There was only one way out of this section of the brewery. Still hobbling, Quincannon went through the boiler room, past the corner room where the vats of rejected beer stood in heavy shadow, then past the freight elevator and down the stairs to the lower floor. An electrically lit passage led into the main tunnel that divided the building in half. He hurried along the tunnel,

out onto the Seventh Street loading dock. There was no sign of
Lansing anywhere in the vicinity. Half a dozen burly workmen
were wrestling filled kegs onto a pair of massive Studebaker
wagons; Quincannon called to them. No, they hadn't seen
Lansing come out.

So his quarry was still in the building. But for how long?

Quincannon's leg still smarted, but he could move more or
less normally again; he ran back inside. Perpendicular to the
tunnel was another wide corridor that led in one direction to
the shipping offices and the main entrance, the other to the cellars. There was no exit from the cellars; he hastened the other
way. But then he encountered a clerk on his way to the dock
with a handful of bills of lading, who told him that Lansing
hadn't gone that way, either. The clerk had been conversing
with another man in the passage for the past five minutes and
would have seen him if he had.

Now Quincannon was nonplussed. He retraced his path along
the side corridor to the brick-walled one that led downward to
the cellars. A workman pushing a hand truck laden with fifty-
pound sacks of barley was just coming up. "Mister Lansing?
Yes, sir, just a few moments ago. Heading into the storerooms."

"The storerooms? Are you certain, man?"

"Aye. In a great hurry he was."

Why the devil would Lansing go there? To hide? Fool's game,
if that was his intention. The storerooms, where all the
ingredients that went into the mass production of beer were
kept, were a collective dead-end. So were the cellar rooms that
housed filled kegs and the enormous cedar vats where green
beer was ripened and finished beer was held before being piped
to the company's bottling plant in a separate building next
door.

Quincannon was not wearing his Navy Colt; James Carreaux
had an aversion to firearms and would not permit them in his

brewery under any circumstances. As he made his way down the passage, he berated himself for not defying Carreaux's edict. Unarmed, he would have to proceed with considerably more caution. Men who blundered into uncertain situations were ripe for suffering the consequences. This was doubly true of detectives.

The temperature dropped considerably as he descended. When he reached the artery that led into the storerooms, the air was frosty enough to require the buttoning of his coat. He passed through a large room stacked on two sides with empty kegs. At its far end, a solid oak door barred the way into the remaining storerooms.

The door, Quincannon had been told, had been installed as a deterrent to both rodents and human pilferage. Years before, a former brewery employee had returned at night and helped himself to a wagonload of sugar and barley, and Carreaux would brook no repeat of that business. The door was kept open during the day but locked at end of shift. Only a handful of men in supervisory positions had keys.

It should not have been closed now. Nor should it be locked, which it was. Quincannon muttered an imprecation. Lansing must have done the locking; he had access to a key. But why? What could he be up to in the storerooms?

Quincannon listened at the door. No sounds came to him through the heavy wood. He bent at the waist to peer through the keyhole. All he could make out was an empty section of concrete floor, lighted but shadow-ridden. He straightened again, scowling, tugging at his beard. The loading dock foreman, Jack Malloy, would have a key; find him, then, and waste no time in doing it.

Just as he turned away, the muffled bark of a pistol came from somewhere inside the storerooms.

Hell and damn! Quincannon swung back to the door, coming up hard against it, rattling it in its frame. Reflex made him tug futilely at the handle. There was no second report, but when he pressed an ear to the wood, he heard several faint sounds. Movement, but what sort he couldn't tell. The silence that followed crackled with tension.

He pushed away again and ran back along the passage until he came on a workman just emerging from the cellars. He sent the man after the loading dock foreman, then took himself back to the door. He tested the latch to make sure it was still locked, even though there was no way anyone could have come out and gotten past him.

Malloy arrived on the run, two other men trailing behind him. "What's the trouble here?" he demanded.

"Someone fired a pistol behind that locked door," Quincannon told him, "not five minutes ago."

"A pistol?" Malloy said, astonished. "In the storerooms?"

"There's no mistake."

"But Mister Carreaux has strict orders against firearms on the premises. . . ."

Quincannon made an impatient growling noise. "Button your lip, lad, and unlock the blasted door."

The foreman was used to the voice of authority; quickly he produced his ring of keys. The door opened inward and Quincannon crowded through first. Two large, chilly rooms opened off the passage, one filled with sacks of barley, the other with boxes of yeast and fifty-pound sacks of malt, hops, and sugar stacked on end. Both enclosures were empty. The sacks and boxes were so tightly packed together that no one could have hidden behind or among them without being seen at a glance.

At the far end of the passage stood another closed door. "What's beyond there?" he asked the foreman.

"Utility room. Well pump and equipment storage."

Quincannon tried the door. It refused his hand on the latch.

"You have a key, Malloy?"

"The lock's the same as on the storeroom door."

"Then open it, man, open it."

Malloy obeyed. The heavy dank smells of mold and earth, and the acrid scent of gunpowder, tickled Quincannon's nostrils as the door creaked inward. Only one electric bulb burned here. Gloom lay thickly beyond the threshold, enfolding the shapes of well pump, coiled hoses, hand trucks, and other equipment. Quincannon found a lucifer in his pocket, scraped it alight on the rough brick wall.

"Lord save us!" Malloy said.

Caleb Lansing lay sprawled on the dirt floor in front of the well pump. Blood glistened blackly on his shirt front. Beside one outflung hand was an old LeMat revolver, the type that used pinfire cartridges. Quincannon knelt to press fingers against the artery in Lansing's neck. Not even the flicker of a pulse.

"What are you men doing here? What's going on?"

The new voice belonged to Adam Corby, the pint-sized bookkeeper. He pushed his way forward, sucked in his breath audibly when he saw what lay at his feet.

"Mister Lansing's shot himself," Malloy said.

"Shot himself? Here?"

"Crazy place for it, by all that's holy."

"Suicide," Corby said in awed tones. "Lansing, of all people."

Quincannon paid no attention to them. While they were gabbling, he finished his examination of the dead man and picked up the LeMat revolver, slipped it into his coat pocket.

Suicide? Bah! Murder, plain enough.

"Murder?" James Carreaux said in disbelief. "How can Lansing's death possibly be murder? He died alone behind not one but two locked doors!"

"No, sir," Quincannon said. "Not alone and not by his own hand."

"I don't understand how you can make such a claim."

"He had no weapon when I braced him in the fermenting room . . . I would have noticed a pistol the size and shape of a LeMat. If he had been armed, he'd've drawn down on me instead of running like a scared rabbit."

"He could have smuggled it in earlier and stashed it somewhere, couldn't he?"

"Plan to take his own his life when he had enough money to flee the city? And do it here in the brewery, in a blasted utility room? No, Mister Carreaux, Caleb Lansing was murdered." Quincannon paused to light his stubby briar, exhale a cloud of smoke. "Three facts prove it beyond a doubt."

"What facts?"

"The location of the fatal wound, for one. Lansing was shot on the left side of the chest, just above the rib cage . . . a decidedly awkward angle for a man to hold a handgun for a self-inflicted wound. Most gunshot suicides choose the head as their target, for the obvious reason."

"I'll grant you that," Carreaux said reluctantly.

"Second fact . . . there were no powder burns on Lansing's shirt or vest. He was shot from a distance of at least eighteen inches, a physical impossibility if his were the finger on the trigger."

"And the third fact?"

"His key to the two doors. It wasn't on his person or anywhere in the utility room. He couldn't have locked that door without it, now, could he?"

The brewery owner sighed and swiveled his creaking chair for a long stare out the window behind his desk. Fog lay over China Basin and the bay beyond; tall ship's masts were visible through its drift, like the fingers of skeletal apparitions. Quincannon, puffing furiously, created an equivalently thick tobacco fog in the office. The good rich aroma of Navy plug helped mask some of the Golden Gate's insidious pungency.

At length Carreaux swiveled back to face him. He was a large man of fifty-odd years, florid, with sideburns that resembled woolly tufts of cotton, and morose gray eyes. Not a happy gent, Quincannon judged, even at the best of times. He said obliquely: "Now you know why I have such an aversion to firearms."

Quincannon made no comment.

"Well, then. You've convinced me . . . murder has been done in my house. Who the devil is responsible?"

"Lansing's accomplice, of course."

"Accomplice?"

"In the theft of Otto Ackermann's formula for steam beer."

"For the finest steam beer on the West Coast," Carreaux amended grimly. "Golden Gate's exclusive formula, until now. I don't suppose there is any chance that Lansing, or this alleged accomplice of his, has yet to turn it over to West Star?"

"None, I'm afraid," Quincannon said. "The charred note and the two thousand dollars in Lansing's flat testify to a consummated deal."

Carreaux sighed again. "I'll try to get an injunction against West Star. But that may not stop them from implementing Ackermann's formula, even with their duplicitous brewmaster in jail."

"You still have the copy of the formula that Ackermann gave you?"

"Yes, in a safe place, but that was years ago. It's possible he made refinements since then. Even if he didn't . . . the competition, man, the competition."

Quincannon understood; he'd been well schooled in the subject. A master brewer's formula, the proportions in which he mixes his ingredients, the manner in which he treats them in the processing, is the lifeblood of a successful brewery. Golden Gate's reputation as San Francisco's best producer of steam beer would suffer, and lead to reduced sales, if West Star were to begin brewing lager of comparable quality.

"Tell me this, Quincannon. Why would Lansing need an accomplice to steal the formula, when he had access to it himself as Ackermann's assistant?"

"The accomplice was likely the brains of the pair. His idea and plan, mayhap. He may even have had a hold of some sort on Lansing to force him into the crime."

"You suspected there were two of them all along, then?"

"Of course," Quincannon lied. He should have suspected it, given Lansing's weak-stick nature. When viewed in the proper light, the man was a poor candidate for the solo planning and execution of such a crime. Ackermann had been a burly gent; it could not have been an easy task to cosh him and then pitch him into that vat of fermenting lager. Well, even the best detectives suffered a blind spot now and then. Not that he would ever admit it to a client, or to Sabina, or anyone else.

"The motive for Lansing's murder?" Carreaux asked. "And why in such a location?"

"My suspicion is that the two arranged to meet secretly in the utility room this morning, likely not for the first time. Lansing was consulting his watch when I found him in the fermenting room, which suggests that the time of a meeting was near at hand. When he escaped from me, he fled to the storerooms to keep the rendezvous and to tell his partner that the game was up. Lansing was the sort who would spill everything in an instant, once he was caught, and the accomplice knew it. Either he felt he had no choice but to dispose of him then and there before his name was revealed, or the killing was premeditated. The latter would explain why he was armed."

"Do you have any idea of his identity?"

"Not as yet."

"Or how he could have committed murder behind two locked doors and escaped unseen with you and others guarding the only exit route?"

"Not as yet. But I'll find out, never fear."

"You'd better, Quincannon," Carreaux said. "You advertise yourself as San Francisco's premier detective. Well, then, prove it as a fact and not mere braggadocio . . . and prove it quickly. For the sake of your reputation and mine!"

The door to the storerooms had been locked again after the removal of Caleb Lansing's body, at Quincannon's urging and Carreaux's order. And all the keys had been rounded up and accounted for. Quincannon took one of the keys with him when he left Carreaux's office. He appropriated a bug-eye lantern from the shipping offices, to supplement the weak electric light, and then let himself into the storerooms and locked the door again behind him.

He re-searched the utility room first, in the interest of thoroughness. It contained nothing that he might have overlooked the first time. He went next to the room housing the sacked barley. The dusty smells of grain and burlap were thick enough to clog his sinuses and produce several explosive sneezes as he shined the bug-eye over the piled sacks. They were stacked close together, at a height of some five feet and flush against the back and side walls. Nothing larger than a kitten could have hidden itself behind or among any of them.

He crossed into the other large room. The boxes of yeast and heavy sacks of malt, sugar, and hops stood in long, tightly packed rows along the side walls. No one could have hidden behind or among them, either. The floor at the far end wall was bare; a pile of empty hop sacks and a pair of hand trucks lay against the near end wall. Everything as it had been when he'd looked in earlier.

Or was it?

No. Something seemed different now. . . .

Quincannon stood for a few moments, cudgeling his memory. Then he made a careful examination of the room and its contents. A thin smile split his freebooter's beard when he finished. So that was the answer! Bully!

He dusted a smudge of yellow powder off his fingers, re-locked the storeroom door, and sought out Jack Malloy. The answers to the questions he asked the loading dock foreman added weight to his conclusions.

Time now to confront his man. Only it wasn't, not quite.

The bookkeeper's cubicle in the office wing was empty. A quick search revealed further damning evidence: a yellow smear on one leg of the desk chair, and two small dried flower buds on the floor under the desk. There could be no doubt now that Adam Corby was Lansing's accomplice, and of how the murder and his disappearance from the locked store rooms had been managed.

He would have proceeded to comb the brewery for Corby, but one of the office staff put a crimp in that notion. "Mister Corby left early," he was told, "not more than half an hour ago. Said he had an important errand to run."

Important errand? Nefarious one, more likely. Well, thirty minutes wasn't too long a head start; if he made haste, he might be able to prevent Corby from completing it and vanishing yet again.

There were no hansom cabs in the vicinity of the brewery. Quincannon had to cover the two blocks to Market Street on shanks' mare before he found one. As he was settling inside, one of the newfangled horseless carriages passed by snorting and growling like a bull on the charge. Dratted machines were noisy polluters that frightened women, children, and horses, but he had to admit that they were capable of traveling at an astonishing rate of speed. Too bad he hadn't the use of one right now; it would get him to his destination twice as fast as the hansom, and speed was of the essence.

At the promise of a 50¢ tip, the hack driver drove his horse at a brisk pace through the crowded streets. Luck rode with Quincannon; the timing of their arrival at Caleb Lansing's boarding house was almost perfect. Two minutes earlier and it would have saved him a considerable amount of temper and exertion.

As it was, Golden Gate's diminutive bookkeeper had just emerged and was on his way through the front gate when the hansom rattled to a stop. Quincannon flung coins at the driver and hopped out. In stentorian tones he roared: "Corby! Adam Corby!"

Corby froze for an instant, his head craned and his eyes a-bulge. Then he emitted a cry that sounded like—"*Awk!*"— and broke into a headlong run.

One foot chase in a single day was irritation enough; two offended Quincannon's dignity and sense of fair play, stoked his wrath. Damned cheeky felons! Growling and grumbling, he plunged after his quarry.

Corby dashed into the street, passing so close to an oncoming carriage that the horse reared. The animal's flashing hoofs narrowly missed Quincannon as it buck-jumped forward. This served to increase both his outrage and his foot speed. The little man was driven by panic, however, and there was still a distance of some twenty rods separating them when he leaped up onto the far sidewalk. He banged into a woman pedestrian, sent her and her reticule flying. Although the collision staggered him, he managed to stay on his feet; seconds later he ducked through the doorway of an oyster house.

By the time Quincannon reached the eatery and flung inside,

Corby was at a counter at the far end and had swung around to face him. Something came flying from his hand, whizzed by Quincannon's head as he advanced, and splattered him with trailing liquid. It was followed by two more of the same—large oysters, unshucked, from an iced bucket on the counter. One of them thumped stingingly against his chest before he could twist aside.

Another indignity! Damn the man's eyes!

Corby spun, raced out a side entrance. Quincannon, unslowed by the hurled oysters, shoved his way through a clutch of startled customers and emerged into a wide cobbled alley. The scoundrel's lead was less than twenty rods now. He threw a look over his shoulder, saw Quincannon gaining on him, and veered sideways across a short yard and through a pair of open doors into a ramshackle wooden building. A sign above the doors proclaimed: Thomas Vail and Sons, Cooperage.

Quincannon pounded inside in Corby's wake. The interior was weakly lighted, inhabited by a trio of men in leather aprons working with hammer, saw, and lathe. Barrels and kegs of various types and sizes rose in stacks along one wall. The rest of the space was cluttered with tools, lumber, staves, forged metal rings. Corby was at the far end, hopping back and forth, searching desperately for a nonexistent rear exit. One of the coopers shouted something that Quincannon paid no attention to. He advanced implacably.

Another—"*Awk!*"—came out of the little man. He dodged sideways, quick but not quick enough. Quincannon clamped fingers around one arm, brought him up short. Corby struggled, managed to tear loose, but in doing so he fell backwards against a stack of barrels; the barrels toppled over on him with a great clatter, knocked him flat to the sawdusted wooden floor. Quincannon danced out of the way just in time to avoid a similar fate.

Corby wasn't badly hurt. He moaned and tried to regain his feet. An extra-solid thump on the cranium changed the little scruff's mind. And a second thump stretched him out cold.

Quincannon was on one knee beside his prisoner, transferring to his own pockets the greenbacks and gold double eagles Corby had taken from Lansing's rooms, when one of the coopers came rushing up. "Here, what's the meaning of all this?" the man demanded in irate tones. "Look what you've done to these barrels!"

Straightening, Quincannon pressed one of the double eagles into his palm. "This will pay for the damage."

The cooper gawped at the coin, then at him. "Who are you, mister?"

"John Quincannon, of Carpenter and Quincannon, Professional Detective Services. At your service."

"A detective?"

"The finest in San Francisco," Quincannon said virtuously, "if not in the nation and the entire world."

It was not often that he could persuade Sabina to dine with him, but he managed it the next day by promising her a full accounting of his prowess in the devil's brew case. Generally his thrifty Scot's nature limited his restaurant meals to the less expensive establishments, but on this evening he surprised Sabina by calling for her in a rented carriage and taking her to Maison Riche—one of the city's tonier French bistros, at Dupont and Geary Streets, whose specialties included such epicurean delights as *caviar sur canane* and *poulet de grain aux cresson*. There were two dining rooms on the ground floor; he requested seating in the smaller, more intimate one with individual tables. He would have preferred one of the discreet dining cubicles on the upper floor, whose amenities included a velvet couch and a door that could be locked from the inside.

But Sabina, of course, would have had none of that and he didn't bother to suggest it.

She had dressed well for him, he was heartened to note. Beneath her lamb's wool coat, she wore a brocade jacket over a snowy shirtwaist and a wine-colored skirt. Pendant ruby earrings, a gift from her late husband, made a fiery compliment to her sleek dark hair. Even more to his liking was the shell brooch at her breast—a gift from her doting partner, bought for her while he'd been away on a case in the Hawaiian Islands the previous year.

When they were seated and their drink orders placed—French wine for Sabina, clam juice for him—Quincannon took one of her small hands in his. "You look particularly lovely tonight, my dear," he said.

She permitted him to hold her hand while she thanked him for the compliment and then gently withdrew it. "Now then, John," she said. "Let's have your explanation."

"Explanation?"

"Of the devil's brew case, as you promised."

"Business before we dine?"

"We both know you've been eager to glory in your latest triumph. You've worn your preening look all day."

"I do not have a preening look."

"Yes, you do. Like a peacock about to crow. Well, go ahead and spread your feathers."

Quincannon pretended to be wounded. "You do me a grave injustice."

"Oh, bosh," she said. "How did you know Adam Corby was guilty of murdering his partner?"

"Lupulin," he said.

". . . I beg your pardon?"

"Yellow glands between the petals of hop flowers. A fine powdery dust clings to them, some of which is released when the flowers are picked." He added sententiously, courtesy of Jack Malloy, that it was this dust, not the hop buds themselves, that offset the sweetness of malt and gave beer its sedative and digestive qualities.

"Amazing," Sabina said, not without irony.

"There was a smudge of the powder on the leg of Corby's office chair. And two dried hop flowers on the floor under his desk."

"Dried? I thought you said the powder comes from freshly picked flowers."

"It does."

"John. . . ."

"Those were the essential clues. Along with two others."

"And what were they?"

"The fact that Corby appeared in the storerooms so soon after we discovered Lansing's body. And the man's stature."

"What do you mean, his stature?"

"Just that. He was the only Golden Gate employee who could have been guilty."

Sabina nudged him with the toe of her shoe, not lightly. "You're being deliberately cryptic. Come now . . . how did these clues identify Corby as the murderer and his method of perpetrating the crime?"

Quincannon fluffed his well-groomed whiskers and adopted a brisk professional air. Sabina was not a woman to be trifled with when it came to business matters; she had been a Pinkerton operative in Denver before he met her, with a record every bit as exemplary, if not more so, than his own. She was not to be trifled with as a woman, either, as he had learned to his frustration and chagrin. Both qualities made her all the more desirable.

"The short and sweet of it, then," he said, and began by relating the same facts and suppositions he had presented to

James Carreaux after the murder. "Corby intended to shoot Lansing at their prearranged meeting in the utility room, had brought the pistol with him for that reason. His motives being self-protection and Lansing's share of the West Star pay-off money. Once Lansing told him that I had accosted and chased him, he wasted no time firing the fatal shot. He placed the revolver near Lansing's hand, rifled his pocket for both the storeroom key and the key to Lansing's rooms. In different circumstances he would have simply unlocked the storeroom door and slipped out at the first opportunity. But he'd heard the sounds I made at the door, knew the shot had been heard and the passage was blocked. He was trapped there with a dead man. What could he do?"

"What did he do?"

"He had two options," Quincannon said. "Hold fast and bluff it out, claim that he'd tried and failed to stop Lansing from shooting himself. But he had no way of knowing how much I knew and he was afraid such a story wouldn't be believed. His second option was to hide and hope his hiding place would be overlooked in the first rush. Corby was quick-witted, I'll give him that. He had less than five minutes to formulate and implement a plan and he used every second. The first thing he did was to lock the utility room door. The same key that operates the storeroom door lock works on that one as well. The idea of that was to create more confusion and solidify the false impression of suicide. Then he entered the room containing the sacks of malt and hops and established his clever hiding place."

"Where?" Sabina asked. "You said you looked into that room and there was no place for a man to hide."

"No obvious place. Corby counted on the fact that the first inspection would be cursory, and that is what happened. If there'd been time for a careful inspection then, I would have found him quickly enough. But I and the others were intent on finding out what had happened to Lansing."

"Well? Where was he?"

"When I first looked in the room, I registered a single sack of hops propped against the end wall. When I returned later, the sack was no longer there. It had been moved back into the tightly wedged row along the side wall. That fact and the pile of empty hop sacks gave me the answer."

"Ah! Corby hid inside one of the empty sacks."

"Just so. He dragged a full sack from the end of the row, climbed into an empty sack, or pulled it down over him, and wedged himself into the space. When Malloy opened the storeroom door and we rushed in, Corby held himself in such a position that he resembled the other sacks in the row. Now you see what I meant by his stature being proof of his guilt. Only a bantam-size man could have fit inside a fifty-pound hop sack."

"And while you and the other men were huddled around Lansing's body, Corby stepped out of the sack, tossed it onto the pile of empties, returned the full sack to its proper place, and pretended to have just arrived."

Quincannon nodded. "It struck me odd at the time that he should have shown up when he did. A brewery's bookkeeper has little business in the storerooms. Unless he'd been there all along and his business was murder."

"The hop flowers you found in his office came from the hide-out sack?"

"Yes. Caught on the twill of his trousers or inside the cuffs."

"And the lupulin?"

"Also from the inside of the sack. Golden Gate buys its hops from a farm in Oregon's Willamette Valley. The flowers are picked, dried, and sacked there, and now and then dried hops are put into bags previously used by pickers. In such cases, a residue of the yellow powder clings to the inside of the burlap. Corby hadn't changed trousers when I apprehended him. The yellow residue was still visible on both legs."

"Well done, John, I must say. But I do have one more question."

"Ask it, my dear."

"I assume you turned the partially burned note over to the police as evidence against Corby. Did you also turn over the two thousand dollars he took from Lansing's rooms?"

Quincannon assumed an injured expression. "And have it disappear into the pockets of a corrupt bluecoat five minutes after I left the Hall of Justice? That would have been irresponsible."

"Which means you still have the money and you intend to keep it."

"And why not?" he said defensively. "It doesn't legally belong to our client or to anyone else. We have just as much right to it as a fat jailer or corrupt desk sergeant. More of a right, by Godfrey, as an added bonus for pure and noble detective work. And I won't listen to any argument to the contrary."

"I won't even try. When it comes to money, John Quincannon, you're incorrigible."

He gazed fondly, longingly into her dark blue eyes. Money was not the only thing about which he was incorrigible.

ANGEL OF MERCY

Her name was Mercy.

Born with a second name, yes, like everyone else, but it had been so long since she'd used it she could scarce remember what it was. Scarce remember so many things about her youth, long faded now—except for Father, of course. It seemed, sometimes, that she had never had a youth at all. That she'd spent her whole life on the road, first with Caleb, and then with Elias, jouncing from place to place in the big black traveling wagon, always moving, drifting, never settling anywhere. Birth to death, with her small deft hands working tirelessly and her eyes asquint in smoky lamplight and her head aswirl with medicines, mixtures, measurements, what was best for this ailment, what was the proper dosage for that one. . . .

Miss Mercy. Father had been the first to call her that, in his little apothecary shop in—what was the name of the town where she'd been born? Lester? No, Dexter. Dexter, Pennsylvania. "A druggist is an angel of mercy," he said to her when she was ten or eleven. "Your name comes from my belief in that, child. Mercy. Miss Mercy. And wouldn't you like to be an angel of mercy one day, too?"

"Oh, yes, Father, yes! Will you show me how?"

And he had shown her, with great patience, because he had no sons and because he bore no prejudice against his daughter or the daughter of any man. He had shown her carefully and well for five or six or seven years, until Mr. President Lincoln declared war against the Confederate States of America and Father went away to bring his mercy to sick and wounded Union soldiers on far-off battlefields. But there was no mercy for him. On one of those battlefields, a place called Antietam, he was himself mortally wounded by cannon fire.

As soon as she received word of his death, she knew what she must do. She had no siblings, and Mother had died years before; Father's legacy was all that was left. And it seemed as though the next thing she knew, she was sitting on the high seat of the big black traveling wagon, alone in the beginning, then with Caleb and then Elias to drive the team of horses, bringing her mercy to those in need. Death to birth, birth to death—it was her true calling. Father would have been proud. He would have understood and he would have been so proud.

Miss Mercy. If it had been necessary to paint a name on the side of the wagon, that was the name she would have chosen. Just that and nothing more. It was what Caleb had called her, too, from their very first meeting in—St. Louis, hadn't it been? Young and strong and restless—there, driving the wagon one day, gone the next and never seen again. And Miss Mercy was the only name Elias wrote on his pad of white paper when the need arose, the name he would have spoken aloud if he hadn't been born deaf and dumb. She had chanced upon him down South somewhere. Georgia, perhaps—he was an emancipated slave from the state of Georgia. Chanced upon him, befriended him, and they had been together ever since. Twenty years? Thirty? Dear Elias. She couldn't have traveled so long and so far, or done so much, if it were not for him.

In all the long years, how many miles had they traveled together? Countless number. North and east in the spring and summer, south and west in the fall and winter. Ohio, Illinois, Minnesota, Iowa, Montana, Kansas, Nebraska, Missouri, Oklahoma, Texas—maybe all the states and territories there were. Civilization and wilderness frontier. Ranches, farms, settlements. Towns that had no druggist, towns that had druggists with short supplies or too little understanding of their craft. Cities, now and then, to replenish medicines that could not be gotten elsewhere. St. Louis and—Chicago? Yes, Chicago. Oh, she could scarce remember them all.

And everywhere they went, the people came. The needy people with their aches and pains, ills and ailments, troubles and sorrows. First to marvel at her skill with mortar and pestle and her vast pharmacopœial knowledge; at the cabinets and tight-fitted shelves Elias had built to hold the myriad glass bottles filled with liquids in all the colors of the rainbow, and below the shelves the rows upon rows of drawers containing ground and powdered drugs, herbs and barks, pastilles and pills. And then to buy what they needed: cough syrups, liniments, worm cures, liver medicines, stomach bitters, blood purifiers. And so much more: two-grain quinine tablets, Bateman's drops, castor oil, Epsom salts and Rochelle salts and Seidlitz powders, paregorics and rheumatism tonics, bottles of Lydia E. Pinkham's Vegetable Compound and Ford's Laxative Compound and Dr. Williams's Pink Pills for Pale People. And, too, in private, with their hands and eyes nervous and their voices low, embarrassed, sometimes ashamed: potency elixirs and aphrodisiacs, emmenagogues and contraceptives, Apiol Compound for suppressed and painful menstruation, fluid extract of kava-kava or emulsion of copaiba for gonorrhea, blue ointment for crab lice.

Mostly they came during the daylight hours, but now and then someone would come rapping on the wagon's door after nightfall. And once in a long while, in the deep dark lonesome night. . . .

"Oh, Miss Mercy, I need help. Can you find it in your heart to help me?"

"What is your trouble, my dear?"

"I've been a fool, such a fool. A man . . . I was too friendly with him and now I'm caught."

"You're certain you're with child?"

"Oh, yes. There's no mistake."

"He won't marry you?"

"He can't. He's already married. Oh, I'm such a fool. Please, will you help me?"

"There, now, you mustn't cry. I'll help you."

"You'll give me something? Truly?"

"Truly."

"Apiol Compound? I've heard that it's rich enough in mucilage to bring on. . . ."

"No, not that. Something more certain."

"Oh, Miss Mercy, you're true to your name. You're an angel of mercy."

And again, as always, she and Elias would be back on roads good and bad, empty and well-traveled. Another town, another state—here, there, no pattern to their travels, going wherever the roads took them. Never lingering anywhere for more than a day or two, except when storm or flood or accident (and, once, an Indian attack) stranded them. And as always the people would come, first to marvel and then to buy: morphine, digitalis, belladonna in carefully measured doses, Dover's powder, petroleum jelly, spirits of camphor and spirits of ammonia, bone liniment and witch hazel, citrate of magnesia, blackberry balsam, oil of sassafras, throat lozenges and eye demulcents, pile remedies and asthma cures, compounds for ailments of kidney and bladder and digestive tract.

And then again, in one of their stopping places, in the deep dark lonesome night. . . .

"Miss Mercy, you don't know what your kindness means to me."

"I do know, child. I do."

"Such a burden, such an awful burden. . . ."

"Yes, but yours will soon be lifted."

"Just one bottle of this liquid will see to that?"

"Just one. Then you'll have no more to fear."

"It smells so sweet. What does it contain?"

"Dried sclerotia of ergot, bark of slippery elm, apiol, and gum arabic."

"Will it taste bad?"

"No, my dear. I've mixed it with syrup."

"And I'm to take the whole bottle at once?"

"Yes. But only at the time of month I tell you. And then you must immediately dispose of the bottle where no one can ever find it. Will you promise?"

"Yes, Miss Mercy. Oh, yes."

"And you must tell no one I helped you. Not even your dearest friend. Will you promise?"

"I promise. I'll never tell a soul, not a living soul."

And again, as always, she and Elias would be away at the break of dawn, when dew lay soft on the grasses and mist coated the land. And sitting beside him on the high seat, remembering the poor girl who had come in the night, she would ask herself once more, as she had so many times, what Father would have said if he'd known of the mixture of ergot and slippery elm, apiol and gum arabic. Would he still think of her as an angel of mercy? Or would he hate her for betraying a sacred trust? And the answer would be as it always was. No, he could never hate her; she must have no real doubt of that. He would understand that her only aim was to bring peace to those poor foolish girls. Peace and succor in their time of need. He would understand.

And she would stop fretting then, reassured of Father's absent pride, and soon that day would end and a new one would be born. And there would be new roads, new settlements and towns, new needs to serve—so many needs to serve.

And one day she saw that it was fall again, the leaves turning crimson and gold—time to turn south and west. But first there was another town, a little town with a name like many others, in a state that might have been Kansas or perhaps Nebraska. And late that night, as Miss Mercy sat weary but strong at her mixing table, her hands busy with mortar and pestle while the lamplight flickered bright, a rapping came soft and urgent on the wagon's door.

Her name was Verity.

Names and faces meant little to Miss Mercy; there were too many to remember even for a minute. But this girl was different somehow. The name lingered, and so she knew would the face. Thin, not pretty, pale hair peeking out from under her bonnet, older than most of the ones who came alone in the night. Older, sadder, but no wiser.

Miss Mercy invited her in, invited her to sit. Verity perched primly on the stool, hands together in her lap, mouth tight-pinched at the corners. She showed no nervousness, no fear or embarrassment. Determined was the word that came to Miss Mercy's mind.

Without preamble Verity said: "I understand you're willing to help girls in trouble."

"What sort of trouble, my dear?"

"The sort that comes to foolish and unmarried girls."

"You're with child?"

Verity nodded. "I come from Riverbrook, Iowa. Do you recall the town, Miss Mercy?"

"Riverbrook? Iowa? There are so many places. . . ."

"You were there four months ago. In June. The second week of June."

"The second week of June. Well. If you say I was, my dear, then of course I was."

"A girl named Grace came to see you then. Grace Potter. Do you remember her?"

"So many come to me," Miss Mercy said. "My memory isn't what it once was. . . ."

"So many girls in trouble, you mean?"

"Sometimes. In the night, as you've come."

"And as Grace came."

"If you say so. As Grace came."

"You gave her something to abort her fetus. I'd like you to give me the same . . . medicine."

"If I do, will you promise to take it only at the time of month I tell you?"

"Yes."

"Will you promise to dispose of the bottle immediately after ingestion, where no one can ever find it?"

"Yes."

"And will you promise to tell no one that I helped you? Not even your dearest friend?"

"Yes."

"Then you shall have what you need."

Miss Mercy picked up her lamp, carried it to one of Elias's cabinets. When she handed the small brown unlabeled bottle to Verity, the girl removed its cork and sniffed the neck. Then Verity poured a drop onto her finger, touched her tongue to it.

"It tastes odd," she said.

"No odder than sweetened castor oil. I've mixed the compound with cherry syrup."

"Compound. What sort of compound?"

"Dried sclerotia of ergot, bark of slippery elm, apiol. . . ."

"My God! All those blended together?"

"Yes, my dear. Why do you look so shocked?"

"Ergot contracts the womb, tightens it even more. So do dried slippery elm and apiol. All mixed together and taken in a large dose at the wrong time of month . . . cramps, paralysis, death in agony. This liquid is pure poison to a pregnant woman!"

"No, you mustn't think that. . . ."

"I do think it," Verity said, "because it's true." She had risen to her feet and was pointing a tremulous finger at Miss Mercy. "I've studied medicine. I work in Riverbrook as a nurse and midwife."

"Nurse? Midwife? But then. . . ."

"Then I'm not with child? No, Miss Mercy, I'm not. The truth is, I have been three months searching for you, ever since I discovered a bottle exactly like this one that Grace Potter failed to dispose of. I thought you guilty of no more than deadly quackery before tonight, but now I know different. You deliberately murdered my sister."

"Murdered?" Now it was Miss Mercy who was shocked. "Oh, no, my dear. No. I brought her mercy."

"You brought her death!"

"Mercy. Your sister, all of them . . . only mercy."

"All of them? How many others besides Grace?"

"Does the number truly matter?"

"Does it truly . . . ! How many, Miss Mercy?"

"I can't say. So many miles, so many places. . . ."

"How many?"

"Thirty? Forty? Fifty? I can scarce remember them all. . . ."

"Dear sweet Lord! You poisoned as many as fifty pregnant girls?"

"Unmarried girls. Poor foolish girls," Miss Mercy said gently. "There are worse things than death, oh, much worse."

"What could be worse than suffering the tortures of hell before the soul is finally released?"

"Enduring the tortures of hell for years, decades, a lifetime. Isn't a few hours of pain and then peace, eternal peace, preferable to lasting torment?"

"How can you believe that bearing a child out of wedlock is so wicked . . . ?"

"No," Miss Mercy said, "the lasting torment is in knowing, seeing the child they've brought into the world. Bastard child, child of sin. Don't you see? God punishes the unwed mother. The wages of sin is death, but God's vengeance on the living is far more terrible. I saved your sister from that. I brought her and all the others mercy from that."

Again she picked up the lamp. With a key from around her neck she unlocked the small satin-lined cabinet Elias had made, lifted out its contents. This she set on the table, the flickering oil lamp close beside it.

Verity looked, and cried out, and tore her gaze away.

Lamplight shone on the glass jar and on the thick formaldehyde that filled it, made a glowing chimera of the tiny twisted thing floating there, with its face that did not seem quite human, with its appendage that might have been an arm and the other that might have been a leg, with its single blind staring eye.

"Now do you understand?" Miss Mercy said. "This is my son, mine and Caleb's. God's vengeance . . . my poor little bastard son."

And she lifted the jar in both hands and held it tight to her bosom, cradled it and began to rock it to and fro, crooning to the fetus inside—a sweet, sad lullaby that sent Verity fleeing from the wagon, away into the deep dark lonesome night.

THE HANGING MAN

It was Sam McCullough who found the hanging man, down on the riverbank behind his livery stable.

Straightaway he went looking for Ed Bozeman and me, being as we were the local sheriff's deputies. Tule River didn't have any full-time law officers back then, in the late 1890s, just volunteers like Boze and me to keep the peace, and a fat-bottomed sheriff who came through from the county seat two or three days a month to look things over and to stuff himself on pig's knuckles at the Germany Café.

Time was just past sunup, on one of those frosty mornings northern California gets in late November, and Sam found Boze already at work inside his mercantile. But they had to come fetch me out of my house, where I was just sitting down to breakfast. I never did open up my place of business—Miller's Feed and Grain—until 8:30 of a weekday morning.

I had some trouble believing it when Sam first told about the hanging man. He said: "Well, how in hell do you think *I* felt?" He always has been an excitable sort and he was frothed up for fair just then. "I like to had a hemorrhage when I saw him hanging there on that black oak. Damnedest sight a man ever stumbled on."

"You say he's a stranger?"

"Stranger to me. Never seen him before."

"You make sure he's dead?"

Sam made a snorting noise. "I ain't even going to answer

that. You just come along and see for yourself."

I got my coat, told my wife Ginny to ring up Doc Petersen on Mr. Bell's invention, and then hustled out with Sam and Boze. It was mighty cold that morning; the sky was clear and brittle-looking, like blue-painted glass, and the sun had the look of a two-day-old egg yolk above the tule marshes east of the river. When we came in alongside the stable, I saw that there was silvery frost all over the grass on the riverbank. You could hear it *crunch* when you walked on it.

The hanging man had frost on him, too. He was strung up on a fat old oak between the stable and the river, opposite a high board fence that separated Sam's property from Joel Pennywell's fix-it shop next door. Dressed mostly in black, he was— black denims, black boots, a black cutaway coat that had seen better days. He had black hair, too, long and kind of matted. And a black tongue pushed out at one corner of a black-mottled face. All that black was streaked in silver, and there was silver on the rope that stretched between his neck and the thick limb above. He was the damnedest sight a man ever stumbled on, all right. Frozen up there, silver and black, glistening in the cold sunlight, like something cast up from the Pit.

We stood looking at him for a time, not saying anything. There was a thin wind off the river and I could feel it prickling up the hair on my neck. But it didn't stir that hanging man, nor any part of him or his clothing.

Boze cleared his throat, and he did it loud enough to make me jump. He asked me: "You know him, Carl?"

"No," I said. "You?"

"No. Drifter, you think?"

"Got the look of one."

Which he did. He'd been in his thirties, smallish, with a clean-shaven fox face and pointy ears. His clothes were shabby, shirt cuffs frayed, button missing off his cutaway coat. We got us a fair number of drifters in Tule River, up from San Francisco or over from the mining country after their luck and their money ran out—men looking for farm work or such other jobs as they could find. Or sometimes looking for trouble. Boze and I had caught one just two weeks before and locked him up for chicken stealing.

"What I want to know," Sam said, "is what in the name of hell he's doing here?"

Boze shrugged and rubbed at his bald spot, like he always does when he's fuddled. He was the same age as me, thirty-four, but he'd been losing his hair for the past ten years. He said: "Appears he's been hanging a while. When'd you close up last evening, Sam?"

"Six, like always."

"Anybody come around afterwards?"

"No."

"Could've happened any time after six, then. It's kind of a lonely spot back here after dark. I reckon there's not much chance anybody saw what happened."

"Joel Pennywell, maybe," I said. "He stays open late some nights."

"We can ask him."

Sam said: "But why'd anybody string him up like that?"

"Maybe he wasn't strung up. Maybe he hung himself."

"Suicide?"

"It's been known to happen," Boze said.

Doc Petersen showed up just then, and a couple of other townsfolk with him; word was starting to get around. Doc, who was sixty and dyspeptic, squinted up at the hanging man, grunted, and said: "Strangulation."

"Doc?"

"Strangulation. Man strangled to death. You can see that

from the way his tongue's out. Neck's not broken. You can see that, too."

"Does that mean he could've killed himself?"

"All it means," Doc said, "is that he didn't jump off a high branch or get jerked hard enough off a horse to break his neck."

"Wasn't a horse involved anyway," I said. "There'd be shoe marks in the area . . . ground was soft enough last night, before the freeze. Boot marks here and there, but that's all."

"I don't know anything about that," Doc said. "All I know is, that gent up there died of strangulation. You want me to tell you anything else, you'll have to cut him down first."

Sam and Boze went to the stable to fetch a ladder. While they were gone, I paced around some, to see if there was anything to find in the vicinity. And I did find something, about a dozen feet from the oak where the boot tracks were heaviest in the grass. It was a circlet of bronze, about three inches in diameter, and, when I picked it up, I saw that it was one of those Presidential Medals the government used to issue at the Philadelphia Mint. On one side it had a likeness of Benjamin Harrison, along with his name and the date of his inauguration, 1889, and on the other were a tomahawk, a peace pipe, and a pair of clasped hands.

There weren't many such medals in California; mostly they'd been supplied to Army officers in other parts of the West, who handed them out to Indians after peace treaties were signed. But this one struck a chord in my memory: I recollected having seen it or one like it some months back. The only thing was, I couldn't quite remember where.

Before I could think any more on it, Boze and Sam came back with the ladder, a plank board, and a horse blanket. Neither of them seemed inclined to do the job at hand, so I climbed up myself and sawed through that half-frozen rope with my pocket knife. It wasn't good work; my mouth was dry when it was done. When we had him down, we covered him up and laid him on the plank. Then we carried him out to Doc's wagon and took him to the Spencer Funeral Home.

After Doc and Obe Spencer stripped the body, Boze and I went through the dead man's clothing. There was no identification of any kind; if he'd been carrying any before he died, somebody had filched it. No wallet or purse, either. All he had in his pockets was the stub of a lead pencil, a half-used book of matches, a short-six seegar, a nearly empty Bull Durham sack, three wheat-straw papers, a two-bit piece, an old Spanish real coin, and a dog-eared and stained copy of a Beadle dime novel called *Captain Dick Talbot, King of the Road; Or, The Black-Hoods of Shasta.*

"Drifter, all right," Boze said when we were done. "Wouldn't you say, Carl?"

"Sure seems that way."

"But even drifters have more belongings than this. Shaving gear, extra clothes . . . at least that much."

"You'd think so," I said. "Might be he had a carpetbag or the like and it's hidden somewhere along the riverbank."

"Either that or it was stolen. But we can go take a look when Doc gets through studying on the body."

I fished out the bronze medal I'd found in the grass earlier and showed it to him. "Picked this up while you and Sam were getting the ladder," I said.

"Belonged to the hanging man, maybe."

"Maybe. But it seems familiar, somehow. I can't quite place where I've seen one like it."

Boze turned the medal over in his hand. "Doesn't ring any bells for me," he said.

"Well, you don't see many around here, and the one I recollect was also a Benjamin Harrison. Could be coincidence, I suppose. Must be if that fella died by his own hand."

"If he did."

"Boze, you think it was suicide?"

"I'm hoping it was," he said, but he didn't sound any more convinced than I was. "I don't like the thought of a murderer running around loose in Tule River."

"That makes two of us," I said.

Doc didn't have much to tell us when he came out. The hanging man had been shot once a long time ago—he had bullet scars on his right shoulder and back—and one foot was missing a pair of toes. There was also a fresh bruise on the left side of his head, above the ear.

Boze asked: "Is it a big bruise, Doc?"

"Big enough."

"Could somebody have hit him hard enough to knock him out?"

"And then hung him afterward? Well, it could've happened that way. His neck's full of rope burns and lacerations, the way it would be if somebody hauled him up over that tree limb."

"Can you reckon how long he's been dead?"

"Last night some time. Best I can do."

Boze and I headed back to the livery stable. The town had come awake by this time. There were plenty of people on the boardwalks and Main Street was crowded with horses and farm wagons; any day now I expected to see somebody with one of those newfangled motor cars. The hanging man was getting plenty of lip service, on Main Street and among the crowd that had gathered back of the stable to gawk at the black oak and trample the grass.

Nothing much goes on in a small town like Tule River, and such as a hanging was bound to stir up folks' imaginations. There hadn't been a killing in the area in four or five years. And damned little mystery since the town was founded back in the days when General Vallejo owned most of the land hereabouts and it was the Mexican flag, not the Stars and Stripes, that flew over California.

None of the crowd had found anything in the way of evidence on the riverbank; they would have told us if they had. None of them knew anything about the hanging man, either. That included Joel Pennywell, who had come over from his fix-it shop next door. He'd closed up around 6:30 last night, he said, and gone straight on home.

After a time Boze and I moved down to the river's edge and commenced a search among the tule grass and trees that grew along there. The day had warmed some; the wind was down and the sun had melted off the last of the frost. A few of the others joined in with us, eager and boisterous, like it was an Easter egg hunt. It was too soon for the full impact of what had happened to settle in on most folks; it hadn't occurred to them yet that maybe they ought to be concerned.

A few minutes before ten o'clock, while we were combing the west side bank up near the Main Street Basin, and still not finding anything, the Whipple youngster came running to tell us that Roberto Ortega and Sam McCullough wanted to see us at the livery stable. Roberto owned a dairy ranch just south of town and claimed to be a descendant of a Spanish conquistador. He was also an honest man, which was why he was in town that morning. He'd found a saddled horse grazing on his pasture land and figured it for a runaway from Sam's livery, so he'd brought it in. But Sam had never seen the animal, an old sway-backed roan, until Roberto showed up with it. Nor had he ever seen the battered carpetbag that was tied behind the cantle of the cheap Mexican saddle.

It figured to be the drifter's horse and carpetbag, sure enough. But whether the drifter had turned the animal loose himself, or somebody else had, we had no way of knowing. As for the carpetbag, it didn't tell us any more about the hanging man than the contents of his pockets. Inside it were some extra clothes, an old Colt Dragoon revolver, shaving tackle, a woman's garter, and nothing at all that might identify the owner.

Sam took the horse, and Boze and I took the carpetbag over to Obe Spencer's to put with the rest of the hanging man's belongings. On the way we held a conference. Fact was, a pair of grain barges were due upriver from San Francisco at eleven, for loading and return. I had three men working for me, but none of them handled the paperwork; I was going to have to spend some time at the feed mill that day, whether I wanted to or not. Which is how it is when you have part-time deputies who are also full-time businessmen. It was a fact of small-town life we'd had to learn to live with.

We worked it out so that Boze would continue making inquiries while I went to work at the mill. Then we'd switch off at one o'clock so he could give his wife Ellie, who was minding the mercantile, some help with customers and with the drummers who always flocked around with Christmas wares right after Thanksgiving.

We also decided that, if neither of us turned up any new information by five o'clock—or even if we did—we would ring up the county seat and make a full report to the sheriff. Not that Joe Perkins would be able to find out anything we couldn't. He was a fat-cat political appointee, and about all he knew how to find was pig's knuckles and beer. But we were bound to do it by the oath of office we'd taken.

We split up at the funeral parlor and I went straight to the mill. My foreman, Gene Kleinschmidt, had opened up; I'd given him a set of keys and he knew to go ahead and unlock the place if I wasn't around. The barges came in twenty minutes after I did, and I had to hustle to get the paperwork ready that they would be carrying back down to San Francisco—bills of lading, requisitions for goods from three different companies.

47

I finished up a little past noon and went out onto the dock to watch the loading. One of the bargemen was talking to Gene. And while he was doing it, he kept flipping something up and down in his hand—a small gold nugget. It was the kind of thing folks made into a watch fob, or kept as a good-luck charm.

And that was how I remembered where I'd seen the Benjamin Harrison Presidential Medal. Eight months or so back a newcomer to the area, a man named Jubal Parsons, had come in to buy some sacks of chicken feed. When he'd reached into his pocket to pay the bill, he had accidentally come out with the medal. "Good-luck charm," he said, and let me glance at it before putting it away again.

Back inside my office I sat down and thought about Jubal Parsons. He was a tenant farmer—had taken over a small farm owned by the Siler brothers out near Willow Creek about nine months ago. Big fellow, over six feet tall, and upwards of 220 pounds. Married to a blonde woman named Greta, a few years younger than him and pretty as they come. Too pretty, some said; a few of the womenfolk, Ellie Bozeman included, thought she had the look and mannerisms of a tramp.

Parsons came into Tule River two or three times a month to trade for supplies, but you seldom saw the wife. Neither of them went to church on Sunday, nor to any of the social events at the Odd Fellows Hall. Parsons kept to himself mostly, didn't seem to have any friends or any particular vices. Always civil, at least to me, but taciturn and kind of broody-looking. Not the sort of fellow you find yourself liking much.

But did the medal I'd found belong to him? And if it did, had he hung the drifter? And if he had, what was his motive?

I was still puzzling on that when Boze showed up. He was a half hour early, and he had Floyd Jones with him. Floyd looked some like Santa Claus—fat and jolly and white-haired—and he liked it when you told him so. He was the night bartender at the

Elkhorn Bar and Grill.

Boze said: "Got some news, Carl. Floyd here saw the hanging man last night. Recognized the body over to Obe Spencer's just now."

Floyd bobbed his head up and down. "He came into the Elkhorn about eight o'clock, asking for work."

I said: "How long did he stay?"

"Half hour, maybe. Told him we already had a swamper and he spent five minutes trying to convince me he'd do a better job of cleaning up. Then he gave it up when he come to see I wasn't listening, and bought a beer and nursed it over by the stove. Seemed he didn't much relish going back into the cold."

"He say anything else to you?"

"Not that I can recall."

"Didn't give his name, either," Boze said. "But there's something else. Tell him, Floyd."

"Well, there was another fella came in just after the drifter," Floyd said. "Ordered a beer and sat watching him. Never took his eyes off that drifter once. I wouldn't have noticed except for that and because we were near empty. Cold kept most everybody to home last night."

"You know this second man?" I asked.

"Sure do. Local farmer. Newcomer to the area, only been around for. . . ."

"Jubal Parsons?"

Floyd blinked at me. "Now how in thunder did you know that?"

"Lucky guess. Parsons leave right after the drifter?"

"He did. Not more than ten seconds afterward."

"You see which direction they went?"

"Downstreet, I think. Toward Sam McCullough's livery."

I thanked Floyd for his help and shooed him on his way. When he was gone, Boze asked me: "Just how did you know it was Jubal Parsons?"

"I finally remembered where I'd seen that Presidential Medal I found. Parsons showed it when he was here one day several months ago. Said it was his good-luck charm."

Boze rubbed at his bald spot. "That and Floyd's testimony make a pretty good case against him, don't they?"

"They do. Reckon I'll go out and have a talk with him."

"We'll both go," Boze said. "Ellie can mind the store the rest of the day. This is more important. Besides, if Parsons is a killer, it'll be safer if there are two of us."

I didn't argue; a hero is something I never was nor wanted to be. We left the mill and went and picked up Boze's buckboard from behind the mercantile. On the way out of town we stopped by his house and mine long enough to fetch our rifles. Then we headed west on Willow Creek Road.

It was a long cool ride out to Jubal Parsons's tenant farm, through a lot of rich farmland and stands of willows and evergreens. Neither of us said much. There wasn't much to say. But I was tensed up and I could see that Boze was, too.

A rutted trail hooked up to the farm from Willow Creek Road, and Boze jounced the buckboard along there some past three o'clock. It was pretty modest acreage. Just a few fields of corn and alfalfa, with a cluster of ramshackle buildings set near where Willow Creek cut through the northwest corner. There was a one-room farmhouse, a chicken coop, a barn, a couple of lean-tos, and a pole corral. That was all except for a small windmill—a Fairbanks, Morse Eclipse—that the Siler brothers had put up because the creek was dry more than half the year.

When we came in sight of the buildings, I could tell that Jubal Parsons had done work on the place. The farmhouse had a fresh coat of whitewash, as did the chicken coop, and the barn had a new roof.

There was nobody in the farmyard, just half a dozen squawking leghorns, when we pulled in and Boze drew rein. But as soon as we stepped down, the front door of the house opened and Greta Parsons came out on the porch. She was wearing a calico dress and high-button shoes, but her head was bare; that butter-yellow hair of hers hung down to her hips, glistening like the bargeman's gold nugget in the sun. She was some pretty woman, for a fact. It made your throat thicken up just to look at her, and funny ideas start to stir around in your head. If ever there was a woman to tempt a man to sin, I thought, it was this one.

Boze stayed near the buckboard, with his rifle held loose in one hand, while I went over to the porch steps and took off my hat. "I'm Carl Miller, Missus Parsons," I said. "That's Ed Bozeman back there. We're from Tule River. Maybe you remember seeing us?"

"Yes, Mister Miller, I remember you."

"We'd like a few words with your husband. Would he be somewhere nearby?"

"He's in the barn," she said. There was something odd about her voice—a kind of dullness, as if she was fatigued. She moved that way, too, loose and jerky. She didn't seem to notice Boze's rifle, or to care if she did.

I said: "Do you want to call him out for us?"

"No, you go on in. It's all right."

I nodded to her and rejoined Boze, and we walked on over to the barn. Alongside it was a McCormick & Deering binder-harvester, and farther down, under a lean-to, was an old buggy with its storm curtains buttoned up. A big gray horse stood in the corral, nuzzling a pile of hay. The smell of dust and earth and manure was ripe on the cool air.

The barn doors were shut. I opened one half, stood aside from the opening, and called out: "Mister Parsons? You in there?"

No answer.

I looked at Boze. He said—"We'll go in together."—and I nodded. Then we shouldered up and I pulled the other door half open. And we went inside.

It was shadowed in there, even with the doors open; those parts of the interior I could make out were empty. I eased away from Boze, toward where the corncrib was. There was sweat on me; I wished I'd taken my own rifle out of the buckboard.

"Mister Parsons?"

Still no answer. I would have tried a third time, but right then Boze said—"Never mind, Carl."—in a way that made me turn around and face him.

He was a dozen paces away, staring down at something under the hayloft. I frowned and moved over to him. Then I saw, too, and my mouth came open and there was a slithery feeling on my back.

Jubal Parsons was lying there dead on the sod floor, with blood all over his shirt front and the side of his face. He'd been shot. There was a .45-70 Springfield rifle beside the body, and, when Boze bent down and struck a match, you could see the black-powder marks mixed up with the blood.

"My God," I said, soft.

"Shot twice," Boze said. "Head and chest."

"Twice rules out suicide."

"Yeah," he said.

We traded looks in the dim light. Then we turned and crossed back to the doors. When we came out, Mrs. Parsons was sitting on the front steps of the house, looking past the windmill at the alfalfa fields. We went over and stopped in front of her. The sun was at our backs, and the way we stood put her in our shadow. That was what made her look up; she hadn't seen us coming, or heard us crossing the yard.

She said: "Did you find him?"

"We found him," Boze said. He took out his badge and showed it to her. "We're county sheriff's deputies, Missus Parsons. You'd best tell us what happened in there."

"I shot him," she said. Matter-of-fact, like she was telling you the time of day. "This morning, just after breakfast. Ever since I've wanted to hitch up the buggy and drive in and tell about it, but I couldn't seem to find the courage. It took all the courage I had to fire the rifle."

"But why'd you do a thing like that?"

"Because of what he did in Tule River last night."

"You mean the hanging man?"

"Yes. Jubal killed him."

"Did he tell you that?"

"Yes. Not long before I shot him."

"Why did he do it . . . hang that fellow?"

"He was crazy jealous, that's why."

I asked her: "Who was the dead man?"

"I don't know."

"You mean to say he was a stranger?"

"Yes," she said. "I only saw him once. Yesterday afternoon. He rode in looking for work. I told him we didn't have any, that we were tenant farmers, but he wouldn't leave. He kept following me around, saying things. He thought I was alone here . . . a woman alone."

"Did he . . . make trouble for you?"

"Just with words. He kept saying things, ugly things. Men like that . . . I don't know why, but they think I'm a woman of easy virtue. It has always been that way, no matter where we've lived."

"What did you do?" Boze asked.

"Ignored him at first. Then I begged him to go away. I told him my husband was wild jealous, but he didn't believe me. I thought I was alone, too, you see. I thought Jubal had gone off to work in the fields."

53

"But he hadn't?"

"Oh, he had. But he came back while the drifter was here and he overheard part of what was said."

"Did he show himself to the man?"

"No. He would have if matters had gone beyond words, but that didn't happen. After a while he got tired of tormenting me and went away. The drifter, I mean."

"Then what happened?"

"Jubal saddled his horse and followed him. He followed that man into Tule River, and, when he caught up with him, he knocked him on the head and he hung him."

Boze and I traded another look. I said what both of us were thinking: "Just for deviling you? He hung a man for that?"

"I told you, Jubal was crazy jealous. You didn't know him. You just . . . you don't know how he was. He said that, if a man thought evil, and spoke evil, it was the same as doing evil. He said, if a man was wicked, he deserved to be hung for his wickedness and the world would be a better place for his leaving it."

She paused, and then made a gesture with one hand at her bosom. It was a meaningless kind of gesture, but you could see where a man might take it the wrong way. Might take her the wrong way, just like she'd said. And not just a man, either— women, too. Everybody that didn't keep their minds open and went rooting around after sin in other folks.

"Besides," she went on, "he worshipped the ground I stand on. He truly did, you know. He couldn't bear the thought of anyone sullying me."

I cleared my throat. The sweat on me had dried and I felt cold now. "Did you hate him, Missus Parsons?"

"Yes, I hated him. Oh, yes. I feared him, too . . . for a long time I feared him more than anything else. He was so big. And so strong-willed. I used to tremble sometimes, just to look at him."

"Was he cruel to you?" Boze asked. "Did he hurt you?"

"He was and he did. But not the way you mean. He didn't beat me, or once lay a hand to me the whole nine years we were married. It was his vengeance that hurt me. I couldn't stand it, I couldn't take any more of it."

She looked away from us again, out over the alfalfa fields—and a long ways beyond them, at something only she could see. "No roots," she said, "that was part of it, too. No roots. Moving here, moving there, always moving . . . three states and five homesteads in less than ten years. And the fear. And the waiting. This was the last time. I couldn't take it ever again. Not one more minute of his jealousy, his cruelty . . . his wickedness."

"Ma'am, you're not making sense. . . ."

"But I am," she said. "Don't you see? He was Jubal Parsons, the Hanging Man."

I started to say something, but she shifted position on the steps just then—and, when she did that, her face came out of shadow and into the sunlight, and I saw in her eyes a kind of terrible knowledge. It put a chill on my neck like the night wind does when it blows across a graveyard.

"That drifter in Tule River wasn't the first man Jubal hung on account of me," she said. "Not even the first in California. That drifter was the Hanging Man's eighth."

CAVE OF ICE

WITH MARCIA MULLER

On the hottest day of summer in the year 1901, Will Reese disobeyed his father's orders and returned to the ice cave. He just couldn't stay away any longer. He had thought about little else but the cave for the past week.

The entrance was at the bottom of a deep, rock-strewn depression on his folks' sheep ranch, one of many such pits in this section of the southern Idaho plain. His father had told him they were collapsed lava cones that had been formed by long-ago flows from the extinct volcano nearby. As Will climbed down into the depression, the temperature dropped with amazing swiftness. At the bottom, near the cave opening, the air had a wintry feel. The coldness was what had led him to the cave that day last week, after he had come here on the trail of a stray Hampshire yearling.

Will donned his sheepskin coat, lit the lantern he had brought, and wedged his tall, lank frame through the fissure into the cave's main chamber. When he stood up, the light reflected in dazzling pinpoints from a hundred icy surfaces.

Ice filled the cave, from frozen pools along its floor to huge crystals suspended from its ceiling twenty feet above. A massive glacial wall bulked up directly ahead, a wall that might have been a few feet or many yards thick. Several natural stone steps, sheeted with ice, led up to a narrow ledge nearby. On the ledge's far side was an icefall, a natural slide that dropped fifteen feet into an arched lava tube. At the bottom of the slide was a jumble of gleaming bones, probably those of a large animal that had fallen down the slide and been unable to climb out.

Will could see his breath misting frostily in the lamplight. He could hear water dripping into the cave from underground streams, water that would soon be frozen. He felt the same excitement he had the first time he'd stood here. An ice cave! He hadn't known such things existed. But his father had; Clay Reese had an unquenchable thirst for knowledge, which he tried to slake by reading and rereading mail-order books on many different subjects. He had told Will about the caves, after Will had raced home with news of his find and brought his father back.

There were two kinds of ice caves, one type found in glaciers and the other in volcanic fissures such as this one. Usually the ice in both types melted in warm weather, but this was one of the rare exceptions. No one knew for sure how or why such caves acted as natural icehouses. Perhaps it had something to do with air pressure and wind flow. The phenomenon was very rare, which made Will's discovery all the more special to him.

His father, however, hadn't seemed to understand this. "I don't want you coming back here again," he'd said. "Now don't argue, Son. It's not safe in a cave like this . . . all kinds of things can happen. Stay clear."

Will had tried in vain to get his father to change his mind. Clay Reese was sometimes difficult to talk to, and lately he had been even more reticent than usual, as if something were weighing on his mind. A fiercely proud man, he had once dreamed of attending college, a dream that had ended with the death of his own father when he was Will's age, fifteen. Disappointment and hard work had turned him into a private person. Yet he and Will had always shared a closeness based on fairness and understanding. Until now, he had always listened to Will's side of things. Will just didn't understand the sudden change in him.

Will spent the better part of an hour exploring. Between the ice wall and the near lava wall was a passage that led more than fifty yards deeper under the volcanic rock, before it ended finally in a glacial barrier that completely filled the cave. Small chambers formed by arches and broken-rock walls opened off the passage. The cave was enormous, no telling yet just how large.

But an hour was all he could spare. He would be missed if he stayed much longer, and he had already been reprimanded more than once this week for neglecting his chores. He made his way back to the main chamber and slipped outside, shrugging out of his coat.

The summer heat was intense after the cave's chill; Will was sweating by the time he reached the rim of the pit. He started toward where he had left his roan horse picketed in the shade of a lava overhang. But then he stopped and stood shading his eyes, peering out over the flat, sun-blasted plain.

Billows of dust rose in a long line, hazing the bright blue sky. Wagons, four of them, were coming from the direction of Volcano, the only settlement within twenty miles. They weren't traveling on the road that led out among the sheep ranches in the area; they were coming at an angle through the sagebrush. And they seemed to be heading toward Will.

Frowning, he moved over next to his horse and waited there, hidden, holding the animal's muzzle to keep him still. The wagons clattered ahead without changing course, and finally drew to a halt at the far end of the pit, where it was easiest to scale the rocky wall. Close to a dozen men clambered down and began to unload lumber, a keg of nails, coils of rope, axes, picks, shovels, and other tools.

Stunned, Will saw that one of the men was his father. Clay Reese, in fact, seemed to be directing the activities of the others. Will also recognized Jess Lacy, proprietor of the Volcano Mercantile, and Harmon Bennett, president of the bank. The other men were laborers.

"First thing to do," Will heard his father say, "is clear a path into the pit so we can take the wagons down there. We'll also have to enlarge the cave opening."

"Dynamite, Clay?" one of the men asked.

"No. Picks and shovels should do it. Then we can start building the ramps and cutting the ice into blocks."

Along with Jess Lacy and Harmon Bennett, Clay Reese disappeared inside the cave. The other men began clearing away rocks, grading a pathway for the wagons.

Will had seen enough. He led the roan away quietly, then mounted and rode out across the plain. His shock had given way to a sense of betrayal.

The town could use ice on these scorching summer days, when cellars weren't able to preserve meat and other perishables; Will understood that. But what he didn't understand was why his father had kept secret his decision to sell the ice. The cave belonged to Will more than to anybody, because he had found it. So why hadn't his father told him about what he intended to do?

Will decided to ask him at dinner.

He rode out to the ranch's north boundary fence to make one of three repairs he had been asked to attend to. By the time he finished, it was too late to make the others; the sun was just starting to wester. He rode on home.

The ranch wagon stood in front of the weathered barn when he arrived, but his father's saddle horse was gone. So were two of the family's three sheep dogs. The other dog followed him into the barn, its barks mingling with the bleating of the sheep in the pens that flanked the shearing shed. He unsaddled his roan, fed it some hay, then crossed to the small sod house under the cottonwoods and went inside.

His mother, in spite of it being the hottest day of the year, was stirring a stew pot on the black iron stove. She turned, her eyes stern. "Will, where have you been all day?"

"I . . . where's Pa?"

"Out east. A ewe and her lamb got through that fence you were supposed to mend and fell into one of the lava pits. Honestly, Will, I don't know what's the matter with you lately. Your father shouldn't have to attend to your chores."

Clay Reese returned an hour before sundown. Immediately he called Will outside and reprimanded him for neglecting to mend the east fence. "The ewe and her lamb weren't badly hurt," he said, "but they might have been killed."

"I'm sorry, Pa."

His father grunted and started to turn away.

"Pa," Will said, "I was at the ice cave today. I saw you come out with the men from town."

"What? I thought I told you not to go there."

"Yes, sir, you did. But why didn't you tell me you planned to sell the ice?"

"Because it's not your business, that's why."

"Pa, it *is* my business. I found that cave. And we've always talked about things before."

"That's enough!" Clay Reese's lean face was flushed. "We won't discuss it. You stay away from that cave. Understood?"

"Yes, sir."

Baffled and hurt, Will tried to bring the subject up again the next day. But his father once more refused to discuss it. Will went about his chores, a sad, empty feeling growing inside him.

Ever since he'd been small, his father had treated him as an adult. The ranch was not a prosperous one, and all three Reeses worked in partnership to keep it going. Yet now his father was shutting him out, and it hurt; it was making him lose respect for a man he had always looked up to. Will couldn't bear that. He began to think of leaving the ranch, striking out on his own.

He could go to a city—Boise, perhaps—and find work. Then,

later on, he could enter college, for his father's thirst for knowledge had been instilled in him, too, and Clay Reese's dream had become his dream. He knew that leaving home would be a form of betrayal, but no more of one than his father's.

He determined to try one more time to talk to the man. It was Saturday noon, and thunderclouds were piling up in the east, when Will approached his father again. Clay Reese was hitching up the wagon for a drive somewhere.

"Pa," he said, "I have to talk to you about the ice cave."

His father's face seemed to cloud as darkly as the sky. "How many times do I have to tell you, Will? There's nothing to discuss. I can't talk now, anyway. I have business to attend to." He climbed into the wagon seat, flicked the reins, and drove off.

Resigned, Will went to his room and packed a bundle. He would leave that night, after his parents were asleep.

The storm broke around 4:00p.m., with thunder and lightning and gusty winds. Clay Reese did not return for supper, and finally Will and his mother ate without him. He had probably decided to wait out the storm in town.

Will spent a restless night as thunder grumbled and rain pelted. It would have been foolish to start his journey in this storm, and, until his father returned, he didn't feel right leaving his mother alone.

Sometime toward morning the storm passed, and he fell into a heavy sleep. It was well past dawn, with the sun blazing again, when his mother awoke him. "Get up, Will," she said. Her voice was anxious. "Your father still isn't home, and I'm worried. You'd best ride into town and try to find him."

"Right away, Ma."

Will dressed quickly, saddled his roan, and rode into the clear, rain-fresh morning. He'd only gone half a mile toward Volcano, however, when he thought of the cave. His father could have gone there yesterday, instead of to town; the ice might have been the business he'd referred to. And it wouldn't take long to check. Will turned his horse off the road and pointed him across open land.

He saw his father's wagon as soon as he came in sight of the lava pit. He sent the roan into a hard run, reined up beside the wagon, and jumped off. There was no sign of Clay Reese, or of any of the laborers, this being Sunday. Will scrambled down the newly graded wagon ramp and ran to the cave opening. It had been enlarged considerably, shored up with timbers. He entered, fumbling in the pocket of his pants for matches.

In the flare of the first match he struck, he saw a jumble of equipment piled to one side; among the axes and picks and coiled rope was a lantern. He used a second match to light the lantern's wick. Now he could see more of the cave—gouges and holes in the once-smooth walls where ice blocks had been cut away; narrow wooden ramps built into the passageway, close to the floor, so that the blocks could be easily dragged out. But there was no sign of his father.

Carrying the lantern, Will hurried deeper into the cave. He went all the way to the solid barrier, then came back and checked some of the smaller chambers. All of them were empty.

He had to fight down panic as he ran back into the main chamber. His father *must* have come into the cave; where could he be? Then Will's gaze picked up the stone steps, the ledge at their top, and the chill air seemed to grow even colder. He climbed the steps, moving as fast as he dared on the slippery surface ice. When he reached the top, he leaned into the fall with the lantern extended.

Down at the bottom of the slide, a huddled form lay alongside the bones of the long-dead animal.

"Pa!" Will shouted the word, shouted it again. But the huddled figure didn't move.

Will half ran, half slid, down the steps and got one of the coils of rope. Back on the ledge, he found a projection of rock and tied one end of the rope securely around it. He played the other end down the fall, tested the fastening, then swung his body onto the slide and let himself down to where his father lay.

Clay Reese was unconscious, but still alive. Will's relief didn't last long, however. Try as he might, he couldn't revive his father. The man had been here all night, lying on the ice. He seemed half frozen. If he did regain consciousness, Will knew, he wouldn't have the strength to climb out by himself.

Will swiftly tied the rope around his father, under the arms. When he struggled back up to the ledge, he tried to pull his father out, but he didn't have the strength to move the inert figure more than a foot or so. He had to have help, yet if he left, his father might die before he could bring men back.

Then another idea came to him, and he wasted no time putting it into action. He got a second coil of rope from below, unfastened the first rope from the projection, and tied the two ropes together to make one long one. When he took the free end down across the cave and outside, he had ten feet left.

He climbed to where the roan stood, caught the bridle, and urged the animal to the cave's entrance. He tied the rope to the saddle horn, mounted, and backed the roan until the rope was taut. Then he and the horse began to pull.

It took agonizing minutes, the roan stumbling a time or two, almost losing balance. But finally the rope slackened somewhat, and this told Will his father had at last been drawn to the top of the fall. Dismounting, he raced back into the cave.

Clay Reese lay sprawled across the ledge. He was starting to regain consciousness when Will reached his side.

He managed to get his father to his feet, then down the steps, out of the cave, and to the far end of the pit where the day's heat penetrated. Exhausted, they both sank to the rocky ground.

Clay Reese gave his son a weak smile.

"You saved my life," he said when the sun began to take away the chill. "I thought I was a dead man for sure."

"What happened, Pa?"

"I climbed those steps out of curiosity, slipped on the ice, and fell down the slide. I couldn't get back out again." His expression turned rueful. "I told you it could be dangerous in there, Will . . . that you shouldn't go in alone. I should have obeyed my own orders."

"Why did you go in alone?"

"To do some exploring, see if I could tell how big the cave really is. If there's enough ice to last another couple of summers, I reckon we'll start making some money."

"*Start* making money?" Will asked, surprised.

"Will, you have a right to know the truth." His father spoke slowly, the words coming hard for him. "The reason I didn't talk to you about selling the ice is that I was afraid to face up to you. I didn't want anyone to know how close we were to losing the ranch. Until you found the cave, I hadn't been able to make the mortgage payments for some time . . . the bank was getting ready to foreclose."

"So that's why you've been so troubled lately."

"Yes. I worked out an arrangement with Jess Lacy and with Harmon Bennett at the bank. Jess buys the ice at a fair price, and I turn the money over to Mister Bennett. The mortgage will be paid off by next summer. Then we can start saving for your college education."

Will was silent for a time; he felt ashamed at having doubted his father. Finally he said: "Pa, I understand now. But I wish you'd told me all of this before."

"I guess I should have," his father admitted. "But my foolish pride wouldn't let me. I'm sorry, Son."

"I'm sorry, too," Will said. "I . . . well . . . I felt like you didn't need me any more. I was going to leave, go off to Boise and hunt work. I'd be gone now if it hadn't stormed last night."

His father grimaced, his face etched with pain. "This has been a bad misunderstanding, Will. From now on, we'll both be honest with each other. As for the cave, well, we'll explore it together next time. And work together on our ice business, too."

"I'd like that, Pa."

Will stood and began to help his father up the ramp to the wagon. As he did, he glanced over at the mouth of the cave— not his cave, but their cave, the family's cave. Then his eyes met his father's, and they both smiled.

Coyote and Quarter-Moon

WITH JEFFREY WALLMANN

With the Laurel County Deputy Sheriff beside her, Jill Quarter-Moon waited for the locksmith to finish unlatching the garage door. Inside, the dog—a good-size Doberman; she had identified it through the window—continued its frantic barking.

The house to which the garage belonged was only a few years old, a big ranch-style set at the end of a *cul-de-sac* and somewhat removed from its neighbors in the expensive Oregon Estates development. Since it was a fair Friday morning in June, several of the neighbors were out and mingling in a wide crescent around the property; some of them Jill recognized from her previous visit here. Two little boys were chasing each other around her Animal Regulation Agency truck, stirring up a pair of other barking dogs nearby. It only added to the din being raised by the Doberman.

At length the locksmith finished and stepped back. "It's all yours," he said.

"You'd better let me go in with you," the deputy said to Jill.

There was a taint of chauvinism in his offer, but she didn't let it upset her. She was a mature twenty-six, and a full-blooded Umatilla Indian, and she was comfortable with both her womanhood and her rôle in society. She was also strikingly attractive, in the light-skinned way of Pacific Northwest Indians, with hip-length brown hair and a long willowy body. Some men, the deputy being one of them, seemed to feel protective, if not downright chivalric, toward her. Nothing made her like a man less than being considered a pretty-and-helpless female.

She shook her head at him and said: "No thanks. I've got my tranquilizer dart gun."

"Suit yourself, then." The deputy gave her a disapproving frown and stepped back out of her way. "It's your throat."

Jill drew a heavy, padded glove over her left hand, gripped the dart gun with her right. Then she caught hold of the door latch and depressed it. The Doberman stopped barking; all she could hear from inside were low growls. The dog sensed that someone was coming in, and, when she opened the door, it would do one of two things: back off and watch her, or attack. She had no way of telling beforehand which it would be.

The Doberman had been locked up inside the garage for at least thirty-six hours. That was how long ago it had first started howling and barking and upsetting the neighbors enough so that one of them had complained to the agency. The owner of the house, Jill had learned in her capacity as field agent, was named Edward Benham; none of the neighbors knew him— he'd kept to himself during the six months he had lived here— and none of them knew anything at all about his dog. Benham hadn't answered his door, nor had she been able to reach him by telephone or track down any local relatives. Finally she had requested, through the agency offices, a court order to enter the premises. A judge had granted it, and, along with the deputy and the locksmith, here she was to release the animal.

She hesitated a moment longer with her hand on the door latch. If the Doberman backed off, she stood a good chance of gentling it enough to lead it out to the truck; she had a way with animals, dogs in particular—something else she could at-tribute to her Indian heritage. But if it attacked, she would have no choice except to shoot it with the tranquilizer gun. An attack-trained, or even an untrained but high-strung, Doberman could tear your throat out in a matter of seconds.

Taking a breath, she opened the door and stepped just inside the entrance. She was careful to act natural, confident; too much caution could be as provoking to a nervous animal as movements too bold or too sudden. Black and short-haired, the Doberman was over near one of the walls—yellowish eyes staring at her, fangs bared and gleaming in the light from the open doorway and the single dusty window. But it stood its ground, forelegs spread, rear end flattened into a crouch.

"Easy," Jill said soothingly. "I'm not going to hurt you."

She started forward, extending her hand, murmuring the words of a lullaby in Shahaptian dialect. The dog cocked its head, ears perked, still growling, still tensed—but it continued to stay where it was and its snub of a tail began to quiver. That was a good sign, Jill knew. No dog wagged its tail before it attacked.

As her eyes became more accustomed to the half light, she could see that there were three small plastic bowls near the Doberman; each of them had been gnawed and deeply scratched. The condition of the bowls told her that the dog had not been fed or watered during the past thirty-six hours. She could also see that in one corner was a wicker sleeping basket about a foot and a half in diameter, and that on a nearby shelf lay a currycomb. These things told her something else, but just what it meant she had no way of knowing yet.

"Easy, boy . . . calm," she said in English. She was within a few paces of the dog now and it still showed no inclination to jump at her. Carefully she removed the thick glove, stretched her hand out so that the Doberman could better take her scent. "That's it, just stay easy, stay easy. . . ."

The dog stopped growling. The tail stub began to quiver faster, the massive head came forward, and she felt the dryness of its nose as it investigated her hand. The yellow eyes looked up at her with what she sensed was a wary acceptance.

Slowly she put away the tranquilizer gun and knelt beside the animal, murmuring the lullaby again, stroking her hand around its neck and ears. When she felt it was ready to trust her, she straightened and patted the dog, took a step toward the entrance. The Doberman followed. And kept on following as she retraced her path toward the door.

They were halfway there when the deputy appeared in the doorway. "You all right in there, lady?" he called.

The Doberman bristled, snarled again low in its throat. Jill stopped and stood still. "Get away, will you?" she said to the deputy, using her normal voice, masking her annoyance so the dog wouldn't sense it. "Get out of sight. And find a hose or a faucet, get some water puddled close by. This animal is dehydrated."

The deputy retreated. Jill reached down to stroke the Doberman another time, then led it slowly out into the sunlight. When they emerged, she saw that the deputy had turned on a faucet built into the garage wall; he was backed off to one side now, one hand on the weapon holstered at his side, like an actor in a "B" movie. The dog paid no attention to him or to anyone else. It went straight for the water and began to lap at it greedily. Jill went with it, again bent down to soothe it with her hands and voice.

While she was doing that, she also checked the license and rabies tags attached to its collar, making a mental note of the numbers stamped into the thin aluminum. Now that the tenseness of the situation had eased, anger was building within her again at the way the dog had been abused. Edward Benham, whoever he was, would pay for that, she thought. She'd make certain of it.

The moment the Doberman finished drinking, Jill stood and faced the bystanders. "All of you move away from the truck," she told them. "And keep those other dogs quiet."

"You want me to get the back open for you?" the deputy asked.

"No. He goes up front with me."

"Up front? Are you crazy, lady?"

"This dog has been cooped up for a long time," Jill said. "If I put him back in the cage, he's liable to have a fit. And he might never trust me again. Up front I can open the window, talk to him, keep him calmed down."

The deputy pursed his lips reprovingly. But as he had earlier, he said—"It's your throat."—and backed off with the others.

When the other dogs were still, Jill caught hold of the Doberman's collar and led it down the driveway to the truck. She opened the passenger door, patted the seat. The Doberman didn't want to go in at first, but she talked to it, coaxing, and finally it obeyed. She shut the door and went around and slid in under the wheel.

"Good boy," she told the dog, smiling. "We showed them, eh?"

Jill put the truck in gear, turned it around, and waved at the scowling deputy as she passed him by.

At the agency—a massive old brick building not far from the university—she turned the Doberman over to Sam Wyatt, the resident veterinarian, for examination and treatment. Then she went to her desk in the office area reserved for field agents and sat down with the Benham case file.

The initial report form had been filled out by the dispatcher who had logged the complaint from one of Benham's neighbors. That report listed the breed of Benham's dog as an Alaskan Husky, female—not a Doberman, male. Jill had been mildly surprised when she went out to the house and discovered that the trapped dog was a Doberman. But then, the agency was a bureaucratic organization, and like all bureaucratic organizations it made mistakes in paperwork more often than it ought to. It was likely that the dispatcher, in checking the registry files for the Benham name, had either pulled the wrong card or miscopied the information from the right one.

But Jill kept thinking about the sleeping basket and the curry-comb inside the garage. The basket had been too small for the Doberman but about the right size for a female Husky. And currycombs were made for long-haired, not short-haired, dogs.

The situation puzzled as well as angered her. And made her more than a little curious. One of the primary character traits of the Umatillas was inquisitiveness, and Jill had inherited it along with her self-reliance and her way with animals. She had her grandmother to thank for honing her curiosity, though, for teaching her never to accept any half truth or partial answer. She could also thank her grandmother who had been born in the days when the tribe lived not on the reservation in northeastern Oregon but along the Umatilla River—the name itself meant "many rocks" or "water rippling over sand"—for nurturing her love for animals and leading her into her present job with the agency. As far back as Jill could remember, the old woman had told and retold the ancient legends about "the People"—the giant creatures, Salmon and Eagle and Fox and the greatest of all, Coyote, the battler of monsters, who ruled the earth before the human beings were created, before all animals shrank to their present size.

But she was not just curious about Benham for her own satisfaction; she had to have the proper data for her report. If the agency pressed charges for animal abuse, which was what she wanted to see happen, and a heavy fine was to be levied against Benham, all pertinent information had to be correct.

She went to the registry files and pulled the card on Edward Benham. The dispatcher, it turned out, hadn't made a mistake after all—the breed of dog listed as being owned by Benham was an Alaskan Husky, female. Also, the license and rabies tag numbers on the card were different from those she had copied down from the Doberman's collar.

One good thing about bureaucratic organizations, she thought, was that they had their filing systems cross-referenced. So she went to the files arranged according to tag numbers and looked up the listed owner of the Doberman.

The card said: *Fox Hollow Kennels, 1423 Canyon Road, Laurel County, Oregon.* Jill had heard of Fox Hollow Kennels; it was a fairly large place some distance outside the city, operated by a man named Largo or Fargo, which specialized in raising a variety of pure-bred dogs. She had been there once on a field investigation that had only peripherally concerned the kennel. She was going to make her second visit, she decided, within the next hour.

The only problem with that decision was that her supervisor, Lloyd Mortisse, vetoed it when she went in to tell him where she was going. Mortisse was a lean, mournful-looking man in his late forties, with wild gray hair that reminded Jill of the beads her grandmother had strung into ornamental baskets. He was also a confirmed bureaucrat, which meant that he loved paperwork, hated anything that upset the routine, and was suspicious of the agents' motives every time they went out into the field.

"Call up Fox Hollow," he told her. "You don't need to go out there. The matter doesn't warrant it."

"I think it does."

"You have other work to do, Miz Quarter-Moon."

"Not as important as this, Mister Mortisse."

She and Mortisse were constantly at odds. There was a mutual animosity, albeit low-key, based on his part by a certain condescension—either because she was a woman or an Indian, or maybe both—and on her part by a lack of respect. It made for less than ideal working conditions.

He said: "And I say it's not important enough for you to neglect your other duties."

"Ask that poor Doberman how important it is."

"I repeat, you're not to pursue the matter beyond a routine telephone call," Mortisse told her sententiously. "Now is that understood?"

"Yes. It's understood."

Jill pivoted, stalked out of the office, and kept right on stalking through the rear entrance and out to her truck. Twenty minutes later she was turning onto the long gravel drive, bordered by pine and Douglas fir, that led to the Fox Hollow Kennels.

She was still so annoyed at Mortisse, and preoccupied with Edward Benham, that she almost didn't see the large truck that came barreling toward her along the drive until it was too late. As it was, she managed to swerve off onto the soft shoulder just in time, and to answer the truck's horn blast with one of her own. It was an old Ford stakebed, she saw as it passed her and braked for the turn onto Canyon Road, with the words *Fox Hollow Kennels* on the driver's door. Three slat-and-wire crates were tied together on the bed, each of which contained what appeared to be a mongrel dog. The dogs had begun barking at the sound of the horns and she could see two of them pawing at the wire mesh.

Again she felt both her curiosity and her anger aroused. Transporting dogs in bunches via truck wasn't exactly inhuman treatment, but it was still a damned poor way to handle animals. And what was an American Kennel Club-registered outfit that specialized in purebreds doing with mongrels?

Jill drove up the access drive and emerged into a wide gravel parking area. The long whitewashed building that housed Fox Hollow's office was on her right, with a horseshoe arrangement of some thirty kennels and an exercise yard behind it. Pine woods surrounded the complex, giving it a rustic atmosphere.

When she parked and got out, the sound of more barking

came to her from the vicinity of the exercise yard. She glanced inside the office, saw that it was empty, and went through a swing gate that led to the back. There, beside a low fence, a man stood tossing dog biscuits into the concrete run on the other side, where half a dozen dogs—all of these purebred setters—crowded and barked together. He was in his late thirties, average-size, with baldhead and nondescript features, wearing Levi's and a University of Oregon sweatshirt. Jill recognized him as the owner, Largo or Fargo.

"Mister Largo?" she said.

He turned, saying: "The name is Fargo." Then he set the food sack down and wiped his hands on his Levi's. His eyes were speculative as he studied both her and her tan agency uniform. "Something I can do for you, miss?"

Jill identified herself. "I'm here about a dog," she said, "a male Doberman, about three years old. It was abandoned inside a house in Oregon Estates at least two days ago. We went in and released it this morning. The house belongs to a man named Benham . . . Edward Benham . . . but the Doberman is registered to Fox Hollow."

Fargo's brows pulled down. "Benham, did you say?"

"That's right. Edward Benham. Do you know him?"

"Well, I don't recognize the name."

"Is it possible you sold him the Doberman?"

"I suppose it is," Fargo said. "Some people don't bother to change the registration. Makes a lot of trouble for all of us when they don't."

"Yes, it does. Would you mind checking your records?"

"Not at all."

He led her around and inside the kennel office. It was a cluttered room that smelled peculiarly of dog, dust, and cheap men's cologne. An open door on the far side led to an attached workroom; Jill could see a bench littered with tools, stacks of lumber, and several slat-and-wire crates of the type she had noticed on the truck, some finished and some under construction.

Along one wall was a filing cabinet and Fargo crossed to it, began to rummage inside. After a time he came out with a folder, opened it, consulted the papers it held, and put it away again. He turned to face Jill.

"Yep," he said, "Edward Benham. He bought the Doberman about three weeks ago. I didn't handle the sale myself . . . one of my assistants took care of it. That's why I didn't recognize the name."

"Is your assistant here now?"

"No, I gave him a three-day weekend to go fishing."

"Is the Doberman the only animal Benham has bought from you?"

"As far as the records show, it is."

"Benham is the registered owner of a female Alaskan Husky," Jill said. "Do you know anyone who specializes in that breed?"

"Not offhand. Check with the American Kennel Club. They might be able to help you."

"I'll do that." Jill paused. "I passed your truck on the way in, Mister Fargo. Do you do a lot of shipping of dogs?"

"Some, yes. Why?"

"Just curious. Where are those three today bound?"

"Portland." Fargo made a deliberate point of looking at his watch. "If you'll excuse me, I've got work to do. . . ."

"Just one more thing. I'd like to see your American Kennel Club registration on the Doberman you sold Benham."

"Can't help you there, I'm afraid," Fargo said. "There wasn't any AKC registration on that Doberman."

"No? Why not? He's certainly a purebred."

"Maybe so, but the animal wasn't bred here. We bought it from a private party who didn't even know the AKC existed."

"What was this private party's name?"

"Adams. Charles Adams. From out of state . . . California. That's why Fox Hollow was the first to register the dog with you people."

Jill decided not to press the matter, at least not with Fargo personally. She had other ways of finding out information about him, about Fox Hollow, and about Edward Benham. She thanked Fargo for his time, left the office, and headed her truck back to the agency.

When she got there, she went first to see Sam Wyatt, to check on the Doberman's health. There was nothing wrong with the animal, Wyatt told her, except for minor malnutrition and dehydration. It had been fed, exercised, and put into one of the larger cages.

She looked in on it. The dog seemed glad to see her; the stub of a tail began to wag when she approached the cage. She played her fingers through the mesh grille, let the Doberman nuzzle them.

While she was doing that, the kennel attendant, a young redhead named Lena Stark, came out of the dispensary. "Hi, Jill," she said. "The patient looks pretty good, doesn't he?"

"He'll look a lot better when we find him a decent owner."

"That's for sure."

"Funny thing . . . he's registered to the Fox Hollow Kennels, but they say he was sold to one Edward Benham. It was Benham's garage he was locked up in."

"Why is that funny?"

"Well, purebred Dobermans don't come cheap. Why would anybody who'd pay for one suddenly go off and desert him?"

"I guess that is kind of odd," Lena admitted. "Unless Benham was called out of town on an urgent matter or something. That would explain it."

"Maybe," Jill said.

"Some people should never own pets, you know? Benham should have left the dog at Fox Hollow. At least they care about the welfare of animals."

"Why do you say that?"

"Because every now and then one of their guys comes in and takes most of our strays."

"Oh? For what reason?"

"They train them and then find homes for them in other parts of the state. A pretty nice gesture, don't you think?"

"Yes," Jill said thoughtfully. "A pretty nice gesture."

She went inside and straight to the filing room, where she pulled the Fox Hollow folder. At her desk she spread out the kennel's animal licensing applications and studied them. It stood to reason that there would be a large number and there were, but, as she sifted through them, Jill was struck by a peculiarity. Not counting the strays Fox Hollow had "adopted" from the agency, which by law had to be vaccinated and licensed before being released, there were less than a dozen dogs brought in and registered over the past twelve months. For a kennel that claimed to specialize in purebreds, this was suspiciously odd. Yet no one else had noticed it in the normal bureaucratic shuffle, just as no one had paid much attention to Fox Hollow's gathering of agency strays.

And why was Fox Hollow in the market for so many stray dogs? Having met Fargo, she doubted that he was the humanitarian type motivated by a desire to save mongrels from euthanasia, a dog's fate if kept unclaimed at the agency for more than four days. No, it sounded as if he were in some sort of strange wholesale pet business—as if the rest of the state, not to mention the rest of the country, didn't have their own animal overpopulation problems.

But where did Edward Benham, and the Doberman, fit in? Jill reviewed the Benham file again, but it had nothing new to tell her. She wished she knew where he'd gone, or of some way to get in touch with him. The obvious way, of course, was through his place of employment; unfortunately, however, pet license applications did not list employment of owners, only home address and telephone number. Nor had any of his neighbors known where he worked.

Briefly she considered trying to bluff information out of one of the credit-reporting companies in the city. Benham had bought rather then rented or leased his house, which meant that he probably carried a mortgage, which meant credit, which meant an application listing his employment. The problem was that legitimate members of such credit companies used special secret numbers to identify themselves when requesting information, so any ruse she might attempt would no doubt fail, and might even backfire and land her in trouble with Mortisse.

Then she thought of Pete Olafson, the office manager for Mid-Valley Adjustment Bureau, a local bad-debt collection service. Mid-Valley could certainly belong to a credit-reporting company. And she knew Pete pretty well, had dated him a few times in recent months. There wasn't any torrid romance brewing between her and the sandy-haired bachelor, but she knew he liked her a good deal—maybe enough to bend the rules a little and check Benham's credit as a favor.

She looked up Mid-Valley's number, dialed it, and was talking to Pete fifteen seconds later. "You must be a mind-reader, Jill," he said after she identified herself. "I was going to call you later. The University Theater is putting on 'Our Town' tomorrow night and I've wangled a couple of free passes. Would you like to go?"

"Sure. If you'll do me a favor in return."

Pete sighed dramatically. "Nothing is free these days, it seems. OK, what is it?"

"I want to know where a man named Edward Benham is

employed. Could you track down his credit applications and find out from them?"

"I can if he's got credit somewhere."

"Well, he owns his own home, out in Oregon Estates. The name is Benham . . . B-e-n-h-a-m . . . Edward. How fast can you find out for me?"

"It shouldn't take long. Sit tight . . . I'll get back to you."

Jill replaced the handset and sat with her chin propped in one palm, brooding. If the lead to Edward Benham through Pete didn't pan out, then what? Talk to his neighbors again? Through them she could find out the name of the real estate agent who had sold Benham his home—but it was unlikely that they would divulge personal information about him, since she had no official capacity. Talk to Fargo again? That probably wouldn't do her any good, either. . . .

The door to Lloyd Mortisse's private office opened; Jill saw him thrust his wild-maned head out and look in her direction. It was not a look of pleasure. "Miz Quarter-Moon," he said. "Come into my office, please."

Jill complied. Mortisse shut the door behind her, sat down at his desk, and glared at her. "I thought," he said stiffly, "that I told you not to go out to Fox Hollow Kennels."

Surprised, Jill asked: "How did you know about that?"

"Mister Fargo called me. He wanted to know why you were out there asking all sorts of questions. He wasn't particularly pleased by your visit. Neither am I. Why did you disobey me?"

"I felt the trip was necessary."

"Oh, you felt it was necessary. I see. That makes it all right, I suppose."

"Look, Mister Mortisse. . . ."

"I do not like disobedience," Mortisse said. "I won't stand for it again, is that clear? Nor will I stand for you harassing private facilities like Fox Hollow. This agency's sole concern in the Benham matter is to house the Doberman for ninety-six hours or until it is claimed. And I'll be the one, not you, to decide if any misdemeanor animal-abuse charges are to be filed against Mister Benham."

Jill thought that it was too bad these weren't the old days, when one of the Umatilla customs in tribal disputes was to hold a potlatch—a fierce social competition at which rival chiefs gave away or destroyed large numbers of blankets, coppers, and slaves in an effort to outdo and therefore vanquish each other. She would have liked nothing better than to challenge Mortisse in this sort of duel, using bureaucratic attitudes and red tape as the throwaway material. She also decided there was no point in trying to explain her suspicions to him; he would only have said in his supercilious way that none of it was agency business. If she was going to get to the bottom of what was going on at Fox Hollow, she would have to do it on her own.

"Do you understand?" Mortisse was saying. "You're to drop this matter and attend to your assigned duties. And you're not to disobey a direct order again, under any circumstances."

"I understand," Jill said thinly. "Is that all?"

"That's all."

She stood and left the office, resisting an impulse to slam the door. The wall clock said that it was 4:10—less than an hour until quitting time for the weekend. *All right,* she thought as she crossed to her desk, *I'll drop the matter while I'm on agency time. But what I do and where I go on my own time is my business, Mortisse or no Mortisse.*

It was another ten minutes, during which time she typed up a pair of two-day-old reports, before Pete Olafson called her back. "Got what you asked for, Jill," he said. "Edward Benham has a pretty fair credit rating, considering he's modestly employed."

"What does he do?"

"He's a deliveryman, it says here. For a kennel."

Jill sat up straight. "Kennel?"

"That's right," Pete said. "Place called Fox Hollow outside the city. Is that what you're after?"

"It's a lot more than I expected," Jill told him. Quickly she arranged tomorrow night's date with him, then replaced the receiver and sat mulling over this latest bit of news.

If she had needed anything more to convince her that something was amiss at Fox Hollow, this was it. Fargo had claimed he didn't know Edward Benham; now it turned out that Benham worked for Fargo. Why had he lied? What was he trying to cover up? And where was Benham? And where did the Doberman fit in?

She spent another half hour at her desk, keeping one eye on the clock and pretending to work while she sorted through questions, facts, and options in her mind. At ten minutes of five, when she couldn't take any more of the inactivity, she went out into the kennel area to see Lena Stark.

"Release the Doberman to me, will you, Lena?" she asked. "I'll bring him back later tonight and check him in with the night attendant."

"Why do you want him?"

"I like his looks and I want to get better acquainted. If it turns out neither Fox Hollow nor Benham decides to claim him, I may just adopt him myself."

"I don't know, Jill. . . ."

"He's all right, isn't he? Sam Wyatt said he was."

"Sure, he's fine. But the rules. . . ."

"Oh, hang the rules. Nobody has to know except you and me and the night attendant. I'll take full responsibility."

"Well . . . OK, I guess you know what you're doing."

Lena opened the cage and the Doberman came out, stubby tail quivering, and nuzzled Jill's hand. She led it out through the rear door, into the parking lot to where her compact was parked. Obediently, as if delighted to be free and in her company, the dog jumped onto the front seat and sat down with an expectant look.

Jill stroked his ears as she drove out of the lot. "I don't want to keep calling you 'boy'," she said. "I think I'll give you a name, even if it's only temporary. How about Tyee?" In the old Chinook jargon, the mixed trade language of Indians and whites in frontier days, "tyee" was the word for chief. "You like that? Tyee?"

The dog cocked its head and made a rumbly sound in its throat.

"Good," Jill said. "Tyee it is."

She drove across the city and into Oregon Estates. Edward Benham's house, she saw when she braked at the end of the *cul-de-sac,* looked as deserted as it had this morning. This was confirmed when she went up and rang the doorbell several times without getting a response.

She took Tyee with her and let him sniff around both front and back. The Doberman showed none of the easy familiarity of a dog on its own turf; rather, she sensed a wary tenseness in the way he moved and keened the air. And when she led him near the garage, he bristled, Jill thought. But then why had he been locked in Benham's garage?

She would have liked to go inside for a better look around, but the locksmith had relocked the doors, as dictated by law, before leaving the premises that morning. The house was securely locked, too, as were each of the windows. And drawn drapes and blinds made it impossible to see into any of the rooms from outside.

Jill took Tyee back to her compact. She sat for a time, considering. Then she started the engine and pointed the car in an easterly direction.

It was just seven o'clock when she came up the access drive

to Fox Hollow Kennels and coasted to a stop on the gravel parking area near the main building. There were no other vehicles around, a *Closed* sign was propped in one dusty pane of the front door, and the complex had a deserted aura; even the dogs in the near kennels were quiet.

She got out, motioning for Tyee to stay where he was on the front seat. The setting sun hung above the tops of the pines straight ahead, bathing everything in a dark-orange radiance. Jill judged that there was about an hour of daylight left, which meant that an hour was all she would have to look around. Prowling in daylight was risky enough, although, if she were seen, she might be able to bluff her way out of trouble by claiming she had brought Tyee back to his registered owner. If she were caught here after dark, no kind of bluff would be worth much.

The office door was locked, but, when she shook it, it rattled loosely in its frame. Jill bent for a closer look at the latch. It was a spring-type lock, rather than a deadbolt. She straightened again, gnawing at her lower lip. Detectives in movies and on TV were forever opening spring locks with credit cards or pieces of celluloid; there was no reason why she couldn't do the same thing. No reason, that was, except that it was illegal and would cost her job, if not a prison term, were she to be caught. She could imagine Lloyd Mortisse smiling like a Cheshire cat at news of her arrest.

But she was already here, and the need to sate her curiosity was overpowering. The debate with her better judgment lasted all of ten seconds. Then she thought—*Well, fools rush in.*—and she went back to the car to get a credit card from her purse.

Less than a minute of maneuvering with the card rewarded her with a sharp *click* as the lock snapped free. The door opened under her hand. Enough of the waning orange sunlight penetrated through the windows, she saw when she stepped inside, so that she didn't need any other kind of light. She went straight to the filing cabinets, began to shuffle through the folders inside.

The kennel records were in something of a shambles; Jill realized quickly that it would take hours, maybe even days, to sort through all the receipts, partial entries, and scraps of paper. But one file was complete enough to hold her attention and to prove interesting. It consisted of truck expenses—repair bills, oil company credit card receipts, and the like—and what intrigued her was that, taken together, they showed that the Fox Hollow delivery truck consistently traveled to certain towns in Oregon, northern California, and southern Washington. Forest Grove, Corvallis, Portland, McMinnville, Ashland, La Grande, Arcata, Kirkland. . . . These, and a few others, comprised a regular route. It might explain why Edward Benham was nowhere to be found at the moment; some of the towns were at least an overnight's drive away, and it was Benham's signature that was on most of the receipts. But the evident truck route also raised more questions. Why such long hauls for a small kennel? Why to some points out of state? And why to these particular towns, when there were numerous others of similar size along the way?

"Curiouser and curiouser," Jill murmured to herself.

She shut the file drawers and turned to the desk. Two of the drawers were locked; she decided it would be best not to try forcing them. None of the other drawers, nor any of the clutter spread across the top, told her anything incriminating or enlightening.

The door to the adjacent workroom was closed, but when she tried the knob, it opened right up. That room was dimmer but there was still enough daylight filtering in to let her see the tools, workbench, stacks of lumber, finished and unfinished crates. She picked through the farrago of items on the bench, caught up slats and corner posts of an unassembled cage, started to put them down again. Then, frowning, she studied one of the wooden posts more carefully.

The post was hollow. So were the others; the inner lengths of all four had been bored out by a large drill bit. When fitted into the frame of a fully constructed cage, the posts would appear solid, their holes concealed by the top and bottom sections. Only when the cage was apart, like now, would the secret compartments be exposed, to be filled or emptied.

Of what?

Jill renewed her search. In a back corner were three rolls of cage wire—and caught on a snag of mesh on one roll was a small cellophane bag. The bag was out of easy sight and difficult to reach, but she managed to retrieve it. It looked new, unopened, and it was maybe 3x5 inches in size. The kind of bag. . . .

And then she knew. All at once, with a kind of wrenching insight, she understood what the bag was for, why the corner posts were hollowed out, what Fox Hollow was involved in. And it was ugly enough and frightening enough to make her feel a chill of apprehension, make her want to get away from there in a hurry. It was more than she had bargained for—considerably more.

She ran out of the workroom, still clutching the cellophane bag in her left hand. At the office door she peered through the glass before letting herself out, to make sure the parking area remained deserted. Then she set the button lock on the knob, stepped outside, pulled the door shut, and started across to her compact.

Tyee was gone.

She stopped, staring in at the empty front seat. She had left the driver's window all the way down and he must have jumped out. Turning, she peered through gathering shadows toward the kennels. But the dogs were still quiet back there, and they wouldn't be if the Doberman had gone prowling in that direction. Where, then? Back down the drive? The pine woods somewhere?

Jill hesitated. The sense of urgency and apprehension demanded that she climb into the car, Tyee or no Tyee, and drive away *pronto*. But she couldn't just leave him here while she went to tell her suspicions to the country sheriff. The law would not come out here tonight no matter what she told them; they'd wait until tomorrow, when the kennel was open for business and when they could obtain a search warrant. And once she left here herself she had no intention of coming back again after dark.

She moved away from the car, toward the dark line of evergreens beyond. It was quiet here, with dusk settling, and sounds carried some distance; the scratching noises reached her ears when she was still twenty paces from the woods. She'd heard enough dogs digging into soft earth to recognize the sound and she quickened her pace. Off to one side was a beaten-down area, not quite a path, and she went into the trees at that point. The digging sounds grew louder. Then she saw Tyee, over behind a decayed moss-festooned log, making earth and dry needles fly out behind him with his forepaws.

"What are you doing?" she called to him. "Come here, Tyee."

The Doberman kept on digging, paying no attention to her. She hurried over to him, around the bulky shape of the log. And then she stopped abruptly, made a startled gasping sound.

A man's arm and clenched hand lay partially uncovered in the soft ground.

Tyee was still digging, still scattering dirt and pine needles. Jill stood frozen, watching part of a broad back encased in a khaki shirt appear.

Now she knew what had happened to Edward Benham.

She made herself step forward, and catch hold of the Doberman's collar. He resisted at first when she tried to tug him away from the shallow grave and what was in it, but she got a firmer grip and pulled harder, and finally he quit struggling. She dragged him around the log, back out of the trees.

Most of the daylight was gone now; the sky was grayish, streaked with red, like bloody finger marks on faded cloth. A light wind had come up and she felt herself shiver as she took the Doberman toward her compact. She was anything but a shrinking violet, but what she had found at Fox Hollow tonight was enough to frighten old Chief Joseph or any of the other venerable Shahaptian warriors. The sooner she was sitting in the safety of the Laurel County Sheriff's office, the better she. . . .

The figure of a man came out from behind her car.

She was ten feet from the driver's door, her right hand on Tyee's collar, and the man just rose up into view like Nashlah, the legendary monster of the Columbia River. Jill made an involuntary cry, stiffened into a standstill. The Doberman seemed to go as tense as she did; a low rumble sounded in his throat as the man came toward them.

Fargo. With a gun in his hand.

"You just keep on holding that dog," he said. He stopped fifteen feet away, holding the gun out at arm's length. "You're both dead if you let go his collar."

She was incapable of speech for several seconds. Then she made herself say: "There's no need for that gun, Mister Fargo. I'm only here to return the Doberman. . . ."

"Sure you are. Let's not play games. You're here because you're a damned snoop. And I'm here because you tripped a silent alarm connected to my house when you broke into the office."

It was not in Jill's nature to panic in a crisis; she got a grip on her fear and held it down, smothered it. "The office door was unlocked," she said. "Maybe you think you locked it when you left, but you didn't. I just glanced inside."

"I don't buy that, either," Fargo said. "I saw you come out of the office. I left my car down the road and walked up here through the trees. I saw you go into the woods over there, too."

"I went to find the dog, that's all."

"But that's not what you found, right? He's got dirt all over his forepaws . . . he's been doing some digging. You found Benham. And now you know too much about everything."

"I don't know what you're talking about."

"I say you do. So does that cellophane bag you're carrying."

Jill looked down at her left hand; she had forgotten all about the bag. And she had never even considered the possibility of a silent alarm system. She had a lot to learn about being a detective—if she survived to profit by her mistakes.

"All right," she said. "It's drugs, isn't it? That's the filthy business you're in."

"You got it."

"Selling drugs to college kids all over the Pacific Northwest," she said. That was the significance of the towns on the Fox Hollow shipping route—they were all college or university towns. Humboldt State in Arcata, Lewis & Clark in Portland, Linfield College in McMinnville, Eastern Oregon College in La Grande. And the state university right here in this city. That was also why Fox Hollow had taken so many stray dogs from the agency; they needed a constant supply to cover their shipment of drugs—cocaine and heroin, probably, the kind usually packaged and shipped in small cellophane bags—to the various suppliers along their network. "Where does it come from? Canada?"

"Mexico," Fargo said. "They bring it up by ship. We cut and package and distribute it."

"To kennels in those other cities, I suppose."

"That's right. They make a nice cover."

"What happens to the dogs you ship?"

"What do you think happens to them? Dogs don't matter when you're running a multi-million-dollar operation. Neither do snoops like you. Nobody fouls up this kind of operation and gets away with it."

Tyee growled again, shifted his weight; Jill tightened her grip on his collar. "Did Benham foul it up? Is that why he's dead?"

"He tried to. His percentage wasn't enough for him and he got greedy. He decided to hijack a shipment for himself . . . substitute milk sugar and then make off with the real stuff. When he left here on Wednesday for Corvallis, he detoured over to his house and made the switch. Only one of the crates had the drugs in it, like always. He had to let the dog out of that one to get at the shipment and it turned on him, tried to bite him."

"This dog . . . the Doberman?"

"Yeah. He managed to lock it up inside his garage, but that left him with an empty crate and he couldn't deliver an empty, not without making the Corvallis contact suspicious. So he loaded his own dog, the Husky, inside the crate and delivered it instead. But our man checked the dope anyway, discovered the switch, and called me. I was waiting for Benham when he got back here."

"And you killed him."

Fargo shrugged. "I had no choice."

"Like you've got no choice with me?"

He shrugged again. "I forgot all about the Doberman, that was my mistake. If I hadn't, I wouldn't have you on my hands. But it just didn't occur to me the dog would raise a ruckus and a nosy agency worker would decide to investigate."

"Why did you lie to me before about knowing Benham?"

"I didn't want you doing any more snooping. I figured, if I gave you that story about selling him the Doberman, you'd come up against a dead-end and drop the whole thing. Same reason I called your supervisor . . . I thought he'd make you drop it. Besides, you had no official capacity. It was your word against mine."

"Lying to me was your second mistake," Jill said. "If you kill me, it'll be your third."

"How do you figure that?"

"I told somebody I came out here tonight. He'll go to the county sheriff if I disappear, and they'll come straight to you."

"That's a bluff," Fargo said. "And I don't bluff. You didn't tell anybody about coming here. Nobody knows but you and me. And pretty soon it'll just be me." He made a gesture with the gun. "Look at it this way. You're only one person, but I got a lot of people depending on me . . . others in the operation, all those kids we supply."

All those kids, Jill thought, and there was a good hot rage inside her now. College kids, some of them still in their teens. White kids, black kids—Indian kids. She had seen too many Indian youths with drug habits; she had talked to the parents of a sixteen-year-old boy who had died from an overdose of heroin on the Umatilla reservation, of a seventeen-year-old girl, an honor student, killed in a drug raid at Trout Lake near the Warm Springs development. Any minority, especially its restless and sometimes disenchanted youth, was susceptible to drug exploitation, and Indians were a minority long oppressed in their own country. That was why she hated drugs, and hated these new oppressors, the drug dealers like Fargo, even more.

Fargo said: "OK, we've done enough talking . . . no use in prolonging things. Turn around, walk into the woods."

"So you can bury me next to Benham?"

"Never mind that. Just move."

"No," she said, and she let her body go limp, sank onto her knees. She dropped the cellophane bag as she did so, and then put that hand flat on the gravel beside her, keeping her other hand on Tyee's collar. The Doberman, sensing the increase of tension between her and Fargo, had his fangs bared now, growling steadily.

"What the hell?" Fargo said. "Get up."

Jill lowered her chin to her chest and began to chant in a soft voice—a Shahaptian prayer.

"I said get up!"

She kept on chanting.

Fargo took two steps toward her, a third, a fourth. That put less than five feet of ground between them. "I'll shoot you right where you are, I mean it . . . !"

She swept up a handful of gravel, hurled it at his face, let go of Tyee's collar, and flung herself to one side.

The gun went off and she heard the bullet strike the ground near her head, felt the sting of a pebble kicked up against her cheek. Then Fargo screamed, and, when Jill rolled over, she saw that Tyee had done what she'd prayed he would—attacked Fargo the instant he was released. He had driven the man backward and knocked him down and was shaking his captured wrist as if it were a stick; the gun had popped loose and sailed off to one side. Fargo cried out again, tried to club the Doberman with his free hand. Blood from where Tyee's teeth had bitten into his wrist flowed down along his right arm.

Jill scrambled to her feet, ran to where the gun lay, and scooped it up. But before she could level it at Fargo, he jack-knifed his body backwards, trying to escape from the Doberman, and cracked his head against the front bumper of her compact; she heard the *thunking* sound it made in the stillness, saw him go limp. Tyee still straddled the inert form, growling, shaking the bloody wrist.

She went over there, caught the dog's collar again, talked to him until he let go of Fargo and backed off with her. But he stood close, alert, alternately looking at the unconscious man and up at her. She knelt and hugged him, and there were tears in her eyes. She disliked women who cried, particularly self-sufficient Indian women, but sometimes—sometimes it was a necessary release.

"You know who you are?" she said to him. "You're not Tyee, you're Coyote. You do battle with monsters and evil beings and you save Indians from harm."

The Doberman licked her hand.

"The Great One isn't supposed to return until the year two thousand, when the world changes again and all darkness is gone, but you're here already and I won't let you go away. You're mine and I'm yours from now on . . . Coyote and Quarter-Moon."

Then she stood, shaky but smiling, and went to re-pick the lock on the office door so she could call the Laurel County sheriff.

THE GUNNY

The old man sat smoking his pipe in the shade in front of Fletcher's Mercantile, one of the rows of neat frame buildings that made up the main street of Bitter Springs. It was mid-afternoon, the sun brassy hot in the late-summer sky, and he was the only citizen in sight when the lanky stranger rode into town from the west.

Horse and rider were dust-spattered, and the lean Appaloosa blew heavily and walked with a weary stiffness, as if ridden long and hard. But the stranger sat his saddle, tall and erect, shoulders pulled back, eyes moving left and right over the empty street. He was young and leaned-down, sharp-featured, a dusty black mustache bracketing lips as thin as a razor slash. Hanging low on his right hip was a Colt double-action in a Mexican loop holster, thong-tied to his thigh.

The old man watched him approach without moving. Smoke from his clay pipe haloed his white-thatched head, seeming hardly to drift in the overheated air. He had a frail, dried-out appearance, like leather left too long to cure in the sun, but his eyes were alert, sharply watchful.

As the stranger neared Fletcher's Mercantile, he took notice of the old man sitting there in the shade. He turned the Appaloosa in that direction, drew rein, and swung easily out of the saddle.

"Hidy, grandpop," he said as he looped the reins around a tie rack. He stepped up onto the boardwalk.

"Hidy yourself."

"Hot, ain't it?"

"Seen it hotter."

"I been riding three days in this heat and I got me a hell of a thirst. You know what I mean?"

"Don't look senile, do I?"

The stranger laughed. "Loaded question, grandpop."

"Saloon up the street, if a cold beer's what you're after."

"It is, but not just yet. Got some business to attend to first."

"That a fact?" the old man asked conversationally.

"Where can I find Sheriff Ben Chadwick?"

"Most days you could find him in his office at the jailhouse, down at the end of Main here. But he don't happen to be there today."

"No? Where is he?"

"Rode out to the Adams place, west of town. Some fool's been running off their stock."

"When's he due back?"

"Don't rightly know. What kind of business you got with the sheriff, son?"

"Killing business."

"So? Who's been killed?"

The young stranger laughed again, without humor. "Nobody yet. Ben Chadwick ain't here, like you said."

The old man took the pipe from his mouth, staring up at the youth. Downstreet somewhere, a dog barked once like a gunshot in the stillness. There were no other sounds except for the faint rasp of the old man's breathing.

"That mean what I think it means?"

"What d'you think it means?"

"Like you're planning on murder. Ben Chadwick's murder."

"Murder ain't the right word. Payback's what I'm fixin' to give."

"Payback for what?"

"Sheriff of yours shot up a couple of men on the trail to Three Forks two weeks ago. You heard about that, grandpop?"

"I heard."

"Well, I was in Arizona Territory when I got word. Else, I'd've been here long before this."

"What was those two fellas to you?"

"One of 'em, Ike Gerard, was my cousin."

"Well, now," the old man said dryly, "lookee what we got here. Johnny Goheen, ain't you?"

"That's right, grandpop. Johnny Goheen."

"Your cousin and his sidekick robbed the bank in Three Forks. Killed a teller. But I reckon that don't cut no ice with the likes of you."

"No, it don't."

"A damn' gunny," the old man said, and spat on the worn boards alongside his chair. "Quick on the shoot, are you?"

"Quick as any there ever was."

"Braggart, too. How many men you shot down, Goheen?"

"Four. All in self-defense."

"Uhn-huh." The old man spat again. "Ben Chadwick's a duly appointed law officer. You kill him, it'll sure enough be murder."

"Will it?"

"They'll hang you for it."

"No warrant out on me. Chadwick draws first, sheriff or no sheriff, I'm entitled to defend myself."

"And you aim to prod him into drawing first."

"If needs be."

"Suppose he don't?"

"He will. Bet your boots he will."

"Maybe he's faster'n you."

"He ain't," Goheen said.

"He's got friends in this town, Ben Chadwick has. They won't let you get away with it."

"You one of 'em? You figure you can stop me?"

The old man said nothing.

Goheen laughed his mirthless laugh. "Tell you what, grand-pop. You sit right here in the shade and rest your old bones. No use gettin' all worked up on such a hot day."

Again the old man was silent.

"Pleasure talkin' to you," Goheen said. He tipped his hat, turned, went upstreet to McQuaid's Resort, and pushed in through the batwings without a backward glance.

The old man sat for a minute or so, staring downstreet to the east—the direction Ben Chadwick had ridden out earlier in the day. The road and the flats in that direction appeared motion-less except for shimmers of heat haze, unmarked by the billows of dust that foretold the arrival of a rider or wagon. Then he knocked the dottle from his pipe, stowed it inside his shirt, and got to his feet. He shuffled over to the Mercantile's entrance.

Howard Fletcher, elderly, balding, his bowtie loosened and his cuffs unbuttoned, looked up from behind the counter and smiled. "Well, Jeb, you get tired of setting out there and decide to come in for a game of cribbage?"

The old man didn't return the smile. "I come in to ask a favor, Howard. You still got that Remington Forty-Four-Forty under the counter? The one I sold you?"

" 'Course I do."

"Cleaned and oiled recently?"

"I'm not one to mistreat a side arm, you know that. Why?"

"I need the use of it."

The curve of Fletcher's mouth turned down the other way. "Now what would you be wanting with a six-gun?"

"I got my reasons."

"Mind my asking what they are?"

"Howard, you and me been friends for a long time and I

ain't never asked you for much. I'm asking you for that Forty-Four-Forty Remington now. I'll get me another handgun somewheres else if you got objections."

"No objections," Fletcher said. "I just don't understand what's got your hackles up."

"You will soon enough. Let's have it."

Fletcher shrugged, reached under the counter, and then laid the blued-steel weapon on top. The old man picked it up, hefted it. Its worn walnut grips fit snugly, familiarly against his palm. Most men he knew, Sheriff Ben Chadwick among them, preferred Colt's single-action Army revolver, but the old man had always sworn by Remington's Model 1875 despite the remnant of the old percussion loading lever under the seven-and-a-half-inch barrel, the side ejector rod, the handle some found clumsy. Colt, Forehand & Wadsworth, Hopkins & Allen, none of 'em made a better or more accurate shooting iron than the Remington single-action—if a man knew how to use it.

He flipped open the gate, made sure all six chambers were filled, and snapped it shut again. "You'll have it back before long, Howard," he said. "One way or another."

"Meaning?"

"You'll find out."

The old man went outside again, the Remington held down along his right leg. The street and the road and desert flats to the east were still empty under the hard sun glare. He hesitated, then walked slowly upstreet toward McQuaid's Resort.

But when he was two buildings from the saloon, he veered off at an angle, stepped onto the boardwalk, and took a leaning position against the wall of Henderson Brothers Feed & Grain. He spat onto the planking at his feet, watching the entrance to the saloon with narrowed eyes. Goheen might do all his waiting inside there, but then again he might not. Be better if he made up his mind to come outside again. If the old man had to go in after him, some citizen might get hurt.

Five minutes he stood there. Ten. Frank Harper drove by, his wagon loaded with fresh-cut lumber. Harper waved, but the old man didn't wave back.

Another five minutes vanished. And then the saloon's batwings popped open and Johnny Goheen appeared, rubbing the back of one thin arm across his mouth and squinting in the direct sunlight. He moved down off the boardwalk, past the hitch rails into the dusty street.

"Hey, boy!" the old man called sharply. "Come over here, boy!"

Goheen's head jerked up and around; he stopped in mid-stride with his hand poised over the handle of his revolver. His face registered surprise when he realized who had called him.

"Grandpop, you better not take that tone of voice with me again. What d'you want?"

The old man shoved away from the Henderson Brothers wall, bringing the Remington up in a level point. When Goheen saw the weapon, his expression changed to one of slack-jawed amazement.

"What I want," the old man said, "is for you to unbuckle your shell belt, slow-like, and drop it."

"You gone crazy?"

"Not hardly. I'm making a citizen's arrest, taking you to the jailhouse."

"The hell you are. On what charge?"

"Threatening the life of a peace officer."

"You can't make a charge like that stick!"

"Circuit judge is a hard man. He don't like a gunny any more'n I do."

"You ain't arrestin' me," Goheen said. "Be damned if you are. Put that iron away, grandpop, or else. . . ."

"Or else what? You'll draw on me?"

"That's right. And I'll kill you dead, too, before you can squeeze off a round."

"Welcome to try, if that's how you want it." The old man lowered the Remington slowly, until he was again holding it muzzle downward. "Well, boy?"

Seconds passed—long, dragging, tense. Goheen's gaze didn't waver; neither did the old man's. Then Goheen said—"All right, by God, you asked for it."—and his hand darted down, came up again filled with his Colt—but when he pulled the trigger, it was only in belated reflex. The Remington roared first and a bullet kicked up dust from his shirt front, drove him half around; his slug went harmlessly into the street. His legs buckled and he dropped to his knees. The double-action slid from his grip; he made no move to pick it up. His face wore the same expression of slack-jawed amazement as before, tempered now by shock and pain.

The old man stepped off the boardwalk and kicked Goheen's side arm to one side. Men were spilling out of buildings along the street, and from behind him the old man could hear Howard Fletcher calling anxiously, but he kept his eyes fixed on the fallen youth at his feet.

Goheen tried to stand, couldn't, and fell sideways, clutching at his bloody chest. Grimacing, he twisted his head to stare up at the old man. "Damn you, grandpop, you hurt me bad. Why? I didn't figure you for no . . . no hero."

"I ain't one. I'm just a retired gunsmith that learned how to shoot fast and straight before you were born."

"Then why? Why?"

"Sheriff's got a bad arm, Goheen. Hurt it when his horse shied at a rattler three days ago. I couldn't stand by and let you kill him. I'd lay my own life down, and gladly, before I'd let that happen."

"What're you talkin' about?"

"My name's Chadwick, too," the old man said. "Sheriff Ben Chadwick's my son."

THE COFFIN TRIMMER

I'm scared.

I have never been so scared.

No one in Little River shares my terror. They refuse to listen to me, to open their eyes to the terrible truth. They call me a superstitious fool. Or tetched, or downright deranged. One day they will realize how blind they've been—the ones that are left. But by then it will be too late.

Lord have mercy on us all.

It doesn't make sense that Little River was chosen. Ours is no worse or different than any other small northern California town. Dairy and beef cattle are what supports us, agricultural crops such as alfalfa, too. We have six saloons, a gambling house, and a whorehouse, compared to only three churches, but that doesn't mean there is much sin or even much impiety. There isn't. We haven't had a killing or any other major crime in nearly twenty years. Rowdyism is confined to Independence Day and once in a while when a cowhand off one of the ranches gets liquored up of a Saturday night. We're a God-fearing town of 1,368 souls, according to the 1892 census. Good souls, with no more than a bucketful destined for a handshake with Satan on their judgment day.

Doesn't make sense, either, that it would start when Abe Bedford put up his new undertaking building. But it did, and no mistake. I used to believe everything that happened in this life had its clear-cut purpose and meaning, and, if you studied on it long enough, looked at it in just the right way, you'd come to know or at least suspect what it was. Not this, though. No one can figure out the cause or reason for this—no one mortal, anyhow. And perhaps that's a blessing. I know too much already; I'm too scared as it is. I reckon I couldn't stand to know the rest of it, too.

Abe Bedford buys all his rough pine boxes and fancier coffins from a casket maker in the county seat. He used to store them in the barn back of his house on Oak Street. Had the coffins trimmed there, as well, by his wife Maude before she passed away, and then by the Widow Brantley; he buys them without lining because it's thriftier that way. His embalming room and viewing parlor were in a rented building down on lower Main, near the train depot. He'd been the only undertaker in town for some while, but Little River was growing and Abe took to fretting that before long some other mortician would move in and open a fancy establishment and take away a good portion of his business. He came to the idea that what he had to do was build his own fancy establishment first, in a better location than lower Main—a place that was big enough for embalming and viewing, and to show off and store his caskets and rough boxes.

So he had a new building put up on the other side of his Oak Street property, close to the street. It had a large plate glass window in front so folks walking or riding by could look in and see the trimmed display coffins with their satin linings and silk pillows and shiny brass fittings. Abe also laid in shrubbery and a lawn and a brick walk and a wide brick drive to accommodate his black hearse and team of four. When it was all done, everybody agreed the new undertaking parlor was a worthy addition to the community.

Abe had been open for business in the new place less than a week when the woman who called herself Grace Selkirk came to town.

No one knew where she came from, or even how she arrived in Little River. She simply appeared one day, and took a room overnight at the hotel where the drummers and railroad men always stayed, and the next day she was living in Abe Bedford's house, keeping it for him and working in the Widow Brantley's stead as his coffin trimmer.

Tongues started to wag right off. Gossip's a major industry in any small town, and in Little River the women and members of the Hot Stove League in Cranmer's General Merchandise Store work harder at it than most. I hear more gossip, I reckon, than just about anyone in town. Cranmer's General Merchandise Store is mine, inherited from my daddy when he passed on fifteen years ago. George Cranmer is my name.

Abe Bedford is a widower and reasonable handsome for a man in his late forties. Grace Selkirk looked to be about thirty-five and was not too hard on the eye, in a chilly sort of way. Before long, folks had Abe and the Selkirk woman sharing a bed. Some even went so far as to claim he had met her on one of his trips to San Francisco, where his son lived, and brought her back with him on the sly so they could live together in sin.

I didn't believe any of it. I've known Abe for four decades; there is no more moral and God-fearing man in this state. He'd heard the gossip, too, and it hurt him. He wouldn't have anything to do with Grace Selkirk, he said to me one night, not that way, not if she was the only woman in 1,000 miles. She made him shiver just to look at her, he said.

I asked him why he hired her and he said he didn't rightly know. She'd showed up on his doorstep the morning after she arrived in town and asked him for the work; he was about to refuse her, for he'd had no trouble doing for himself since Maude died, but he couldn't seem to find the words. Couldn't bring himself to let her go since, either. She was a good cook and housekeeper, he said, and the fact was she trimmed coffins better than Maude or the Widow Brantley ever had. Why, some of her finished caskets were funerary works of art.

Nobody liked Grace Selkirk much. She never made any effort to be neighborly and little enough to be civil. Stayed close to Abe's home and undertaking parlor, and, on the few occasions she came down to Main Street and into my store, she hardly spoke a word. I could surely understand why she made Abe shiver. She was the coldest woman I'd ever laid eyes on. Ice and snow weren't any colder.

One blustery day when she walked into the store, old Mead Downey was occupying his usual stool by the white-bellied stove, and he tried to make conversation with her. She wouldn't have any of it. Went about her business and then walked out as if old Mead wasn't even there. He spit against the hot side of the stove, waited for it to sizzle, and allowed as how he'd never believed those rumors about her and Abe and now he knowed for a fact they weren't true.

"Why's that?" one of the other loafers asked him.

"He's still alive, ain't he?" Mead said. "First time he stuck his pizzle in that woman, him and it would've froze solid."

All the boys laughed fit to choke. I laughed, too. I thought it was a pretty funny remark then.

It isn't funny now.

The one thing about Grace Selkirk that you couldn't fault was her coffin-trimming. As Abe had said, she was an artist with silk and satin, taking pains to get the folds in the lining and the fluff of the pillows just so. She did her work right there in the showroom, in plain sight behind the plate glass window. Most any time of day, and late some evenings, you'd see her at it. She spent twice as much time working in the undertaking building as she did keeping Abe's house for him.

It wasn't that she was readying caskets for future use. No, all the ones she trimmed were for fresh business. More folks than usual had commenced dying in Little River. Nobody worried about the increase in fatalities; births and deaths run that way, in high-low cycles. A feeble joke even got started that Abe had done such a bang-up job on his new establishment, people were dying to get into it.

Grace Selkirk had been in town about six weeks when Charley Bluegrass came rushing into my store one night. It was a chilly fall night with a touch of rain in the air. I'd stayed open late, as I often do, because I am a confirmed bachelor and I'd rather be in the store playing checkers and dominoes and shooting the breeze with members of the Hot Stove League than sitting alone in my dusty parlor.

Bluegrass wasn't Charley's true last name. Everyone called him that on account of he'd planted a Kentucky Bluegrass lawn for Miss Edna Tolliver a few years back and it had come up so rich and green, half the women in the county took after him to do the same job for them. Which he did. He'd given up his handyman chores and taken to working as a gardener full-time. Charley was a half-breed Miwok and liked his liquor more than most men. He'd been liking it pretty well on this night; you could smell it on him when he blew in.

He was all het up, his eyes sparkly with drink and excitement. "That new woman, that Grace Selkirk . . . she's dead!"

The Hot Stove League and I all came to attention. I said: "Dead? You sure, Charley?"

"I'm sure. I seen her through the window at the undertaker's. All laid out in one of them coffins, deader than a doornail."

Frank McGee crossed himself. He was new in town and a freshman member of the league, a young clerk in the Argonaut Drugstore who drove his wagon all the way to the county seat of a Sunday so he and his wife could attend what he called Mass in the Catholic Church over there. Old Mead said—"What killed her? Frostbite?"—and commenced to cackling like a hen with a half-stuck egg. Nobody paid him any mind.

"I don't know what killed her," Charley Bluegrass said. "I didn't see no marks, no blood or nothing, but I didn't stop to look close."

"Some of you gents better go on over to the undertaking parlor and have a look," I said. "And then tell Abe."

Toby Harper and Evan Millhauser volunteered and hurried out. Charley Bluegrass stayed behind to warm himself at the stove and sneak another drink from the flask he carried in his hip pocket. I don't usually allow the imbibing of spirits on the premises—I don't drink or smoke myself; chewing sassafras root is my only vice—but under the circumstances I figured Charley was entitled.

We all thought Toby and Evan would be gone a while, but they were back in ten minutes. And laughing when they walked in. "False alarm," Toby said. "That Selkirk woman ain't dead. She's walking around over there, livelier than any gent in this room."

Charley Bluegrass jumped to his feet. "That can't be. She's dead. I saw her laid out in that coffin."

"Well, she just got resurrected," Evan said. "You better change the brand of panther piss you're drinking, Charley. It's making you see things that aren't there."

Charley shook his head. "I tell you, she was dead. The lamp-light was real bright. Her face . . . it was all white and waxy. Something strange, too, like it wasn't. . . ." He bit the last word off and swallowed the ones that would have come next. A shiver went through him; he reached for his flask.

"Like it wasn't what?" I asked him.

"No," he said, "no, I ain't going to say."

Toby said: "I'll bet she was lining the coffin and laid down in it to try it for a fit. You know how she is with her trimming. Everything's got to be just so."

"Tired, too, probably, hard as she works," one of the others said. "Felt so good, stretched out on all that silk and satin, she fell asleep. That's what you saw, Charley. Her sleeping in that box."

"She wasn't sleeping," Charley Bluegrass said, "she was dead." And nobody could convince him otherwise.

The next morning he was the one who was dead.

Heart failure, Doc Miller said. Charley Bluegrass was thirty-seven years old and never sick a day in his life.

Citizens of Little River kept right on dying. Old folks, middle-aged, young, even kids and infants. More all the time, though not so many more that it was alarming. Wasn't like a plague or an epidemic. No, what they died of was the same ailments and frailties and carelessness as always. Pneumonia, whooping cough, diphtheria, coronary thrombosis, consumption, cancer, colic, heart failure, old age, accident and misadventure. Only odd fact was that more deaths than usual seemed to be sudden, of people like Charley Bluegrass that hadn't been sick or frail. Old Mead was one who just up and died. The young Catholic clerk, Frank McGee, was another.

When I heard about Frank, I took over to the undertaking parlor to pay my respects. Mrs. McGee was there, grieving next to the casket. I told her how sorry I was, and she said: "Thank you, Mister Cranmer. It was so sudden . . . I just don't understand it. Last night my Frank was fine. Why, he even laughed about dying before his time."

"Laughed?"

"Well, you recollect what happened to that half-breed Indian, Charley Bluegrass? The night before he died?"

"I surely do."

"Same curious thing happened to my Frank. He went out for a walk after supper and chanced over here to Oak Street. When he looked in through Mister Bedford's show window, he saw the very same as Charley Bluegrass."

"You mean Grace Selkirk lying in one of the coffins?"

"I do," Mrs. McGee said. "Frank thought she was dead. There was something peculiar about her face, he said."

"Peculiar how?"

"He wouldn't tell me. Whatever it was, it bothered him some."

Charley Bluegrass, I recalled, had also remarked about Grace Selkirk's face. And he hadn't wanted to talk about what it was, either.

"Frank was solemn and quiet for a time. But not long. You know how cheerful he always was, Mister Cranmer. He rallied and said he must've been wrong and she was asleep. Either that, or he'd had a delusion . . . and him not even a drinking man. Then he laughed and said he hoped he wouldn't end up dead before his time like poor Charley Bluegrass. . . ." She broke off, weeping.

Right then, I began to get a glimmer of the truth.

Almost everyone in Little River visited my store of a week. Whenever a spouse or relative or close acquaintance of the recent deceased came in, I took the lady or gent aside and asked questions. Three told me the same as Frank McGee's widow. Their dead had also chanced by the undertaking parlor not long before they drew their last breaths, and through the show window saw Grace Selkirk lying in one of the coffins, dead or asleep. Two of the deceased had mentioned her face, too— something not quite right about it that had disturbed them but that they wouldn't discuss.

Five was too many for coincidence. If there was that many admitted what they'd seen, it was likely an equal number—and perhaps quite a few more than that—had kept it to themselves, taken it with them to their graves.

That was when I knew for certain.

My first impulse was to rush over and confront Grace Selkirk straight out. But it would have been pure folly and I came to my senses before I gave in to it. I went to see Abe Bedford instead. He was my best friend, and I thought, if anybody in town would listen to me, it was Abe.

I was wrong. He backed off from me same as if I'd just told him I was a leper. Why, it was the most ridiculous thing he'd ever heard, he said. I must be deranged to put stock in such an evil notion. Drive her out of town? Take a rope or a gun to her? "You go around urging such violence against a poor spinster, George Cranmer," he said, "and you'll be the one driven out of town."

He was nearly right, too. The ministers of our three churches wouldn't listen, nor would the mayor or the town council or anyone else in Little River. The truth was too dreadful for them to credit; they shut their minds to it. Folks stopped trading at my store, commenced to shunning me on the street. Wasn't anything I could do or say to turn even one person to my way of thinking.

Finally I quit trying and put pen to paper and wrote it all out here. I pray someone will read it later on, someone outside Little River, and believe it for the pure gospel truth it is. I have no other hope left than that.

She calls herself Grace Selkirk but that isn't her name. She has no name, Christian or otherwise. She isn't a mortal woman. And coffin trimming isn't just work she's good at—it's her true work, it's what she is. The Coffin Trimmer.

The Angel of Death.

I don't know if she's after the whole town, every last soul in Little River, but I suspect she is. Might get them, too. One other fact I do know. This isn't the first town she's come to and it won't be the last. Makes a body tremble to think how many must have come before, all over the country, all over the world, and how many will come after.

But that is not the real reason I'm so scared. No, not even that. Last night I worked late and walked home by way of Oak Street. Couldn't help myself, any more than I could help glancing through Abe Bedford's show window. And there she was in a fresh-trimmed coffin, the silk and satin draped just so around her, face all pale and waxy and dead. But the face wasn't hers; I looked at it close to make sure.

It was mine. A shadow vision of my own fresh corpse waiting to be put into the ground.

I'm next.

MAN ON THE RUN

When Harry Dice finally caught up with me, I was in Washington state, working the cranberry bogs on the Long Beach peninsula.

It was mid-October and I'd been there nearly three months, at least a month longer than it was safe to stay in any one place. A big mistake to hang on that long, but there were reasons why I'd done it. I was tired of running, that was one. Another: I hated having to leave Anne, the first woman I'd cared anything about since Fay. Another: I didn't want to let Ev Cotter down; the cranberry harvest was due in a week, and the growers needed all the help they could get. Another: Long Beach was the first place I'd been in twenty-nine years of rambling and scrambling that felt like a home to me.

Cold, the morning Dice showed up. Blustery wind off the Pacific, whipping across the peninsula to rumple the surface of Shoalwater Bay. The land finger is fourteen miles long, but only about two miles wide for most of its length; if it weren't flattish and heavily wooded with pine and cedar, you could stand in the middle of it and see both the long stretches of beach on the ocean side and the Shoalwater and Willapa Bay shorelines on the inland side. The locals call it "Cape Cod of the West", because of its shape and the cranberries and a heavy summer population.

I was out in Cotter's bogs, on the slender levee road between #6 field and #7 field, finishing up the last of the mowing. The sunken bogs were all reddish stubble now, ready for next week's flooding and harvesting. The cranberry harvest is a big deal in Long Beach; 550 acres of cranberries are grown on the peninsula, almost ten percent of the entire West Coast production. I was looking forward to it. If you'd said to me three or four years ago that before I turned thirty I'd get a kick out of standing hip-deep in freezing water, scooping off floating berries with a long wooden paddle, I'd have laughed in your face. Rambling and scrambling changes people, I guess. Or maybe it's just that it takes some a hell of a lot longer than others to grow up.

I thought about Anne as I worked. She was a schoolteacher in Oysterville, the village on the northern tip; I'd met her in a supermarket two weeks after I hit Long Beach. And she was about as different from Fay as it was possible for two women to be. Anne was sweet, warm, gentle. Fay had been beautiful, hot, and hard—fire burning around a core of ice. Anne didn't smoke or drink; Fay had been a chain-smoker and an alcoholic. Anne did charity and volunteer work, cared about people, and wasn't much interested in the things money could buy. Fay hadn't given a damn about anybody but herself, took what she wanted when she wanted it, and loved the power of the almighty dollar as much as she loved Fay Dice.

With her it had been secret meetings and secret plans and body heat. With Anne it was movies, dinners, walks along the beach, sail boating on Willapa Bay—and a good night kiss when I took her home. I'd have laughed in your face once, too, if you'd told me a good night kiss and holding hands would be enough for me with any woman. It was best for Anne that things hadn't gotten too serious between us, but I regretted it just the same. And pretty soon now, despite how I felt, I'd have to leave her cold—no explanations, no good byes. It would hurt her, but what choice did I have? A man on the run. . . .

"Hello, Maguire."

He said it loud, to make himself heard over the *whine* of the mower. I swung around and there he was, five feet away. Just standing there, all alone, watching me. Harry Dice.

A chill went up my back. In those first few seconds I had a crazy urge to cut and run, keep on running until he caught me or I dropped from exhaustion. But there was nowhere to go, not any more. When the panic died, I didn't feel much of anything. Funny. I'd had nightmares about coming face to face with him like this, and each time I'd woken up dripping with fear sweat. Now that the moment had come, I wasn't afraid. The only feeling in me seemed to be a kind of distant relief that this part of it was finally over.

I shut off the mower. After that, neither of us moved for maybe a minute. Harry Dice. Big shot criminal lawyer. Mob lawyer, with ties to one of the worst crime families in the Chicago area—but I hadn't known that until it was too late. I'd had contact with him less than a dozen times in Chicago, for about a minute each. We'd said less than 100 words to each other; men like Dice don't have conversations with the attendants who park their cars. In my memory I'd built him up as a big man, imposing, powerful, a giant with eyes that could slice you up like knives—and he was none of those things. Just a middle-aged man in a camel's hair overcoat, hunch-shouldered, with saggy jowls and creases in his cheeks and eyes that were squinty and moist from the wind. Harry Dice in the flesh wasn't any less deadly, a little easier to face was all, especially since he hadn't brought anybody with him.

"You don't seem surprised to see me," he said. His voice was powerful enough—he was supposed to be hell on wheels in a courtroom—but there was a flatness, almost a dullness to the words. He had every reason to hate my guts, but there was no hate in his tone. Maybe that meant something. And maybe it didn't.

"No. The odds were all on your side, Mister Dice."

"Three years is a long time to keep running."

"I figured it was better than the alternative."

"Easier on both of us if you hadn't managed to stay one jump ahead of the detectives I hired. They came close to grabbing you twice the first year."

"Detectives?" I said. "Is that what they were?"

"What did you think they were?"

I didn't say anything.

"You never stayed anywhere longer than two months," Dice said, "and yet you've been here almost three. I wonder why."

"I like it here."

"Is that the only reason?"

When I didn't answer, he said: "Born in Chicago, weren't you?"

In a south side slum. "You know where I was born, Mister Dice."

"City boy," he said. "Urban environment most of your life until three years ago. I expected you to try losing yourself in a city, but the only one you've been to is Seattle for a couple of weeks."

"I guess I had enough of city living." And city people like Fay. And Harry Dice. And guys I grew up with who used crack and smack and died with bullets in their heads. And my mother, who never even knew my father's name.

"Cranberry bogs," he said, and shook his head. "There can't be much money in a job like this."

"Hardly any. But money isn't everything."

"You must have thought it was once, three years ago."

"Look, Mister Dice. . . ."

"Fifteen or sixteen jobs since you left Chicago, and every one menial. Took you two years to scrape together enough to buy that beat-up old Ford you drive."

"I never got any of that eighty-five thousand," I said. "Fay took it all when she left me. It burned up with her in the accident."

Noise had begun to fill the gray sky—*honking* and fluttering. It made Dice look up. Flock of Canada geese, flying in formation the way they always did, headed up over Shoalwater Bay for the wild-life refuge on Long Island. He watched them for a few seconds before he put his eyes on me again.

"I don't give a damn about the money," he said.

". . . You don't?"

"I never did."

"But I thought. . . ."

"I don't care what you thought. Tell me, Maguire . . . where were you when Fay died?"

My lips were dry from the wind. I licked them before I said: "On a bus halfway between Denver and Salt Lake City."

"So it was over between you and her by then?"

"All over. Finished."

"The car she was driving . . . you bought it in upstate Illinois in your name."

"I bought it, but she gave me the cash."

"And you let her take it in Denver. The car and the eighty-five thousand. Just like that."

"There wasn't any other choice."

His mouth opened, started to shape a word—the first one of a question, maybe. Then he seemed to shake himself. When he spoke again, I had the feeling it wasn't what he'd been about to say before.

"The two of you didn't even last a week together."

"No, not even a week."

"How long were you sleeping with her in Chicago?"

"Six weeks. Seven. I don't remember."

"It meant that little to you?"

"It meant plenty in the beginning."

"Did it? Were you in love with her?"

"I thought I was. I mean that, Mister Dice."

"Was she in love with you?"

"Same thing. She thought she was, or tried to talk herself into believing she was."

"Whose idea for the two of you to run off together?"

"Hers."

"Whose idea to take the money out of my safe?"

"Hers. I didn't know it was so much until we got to Denver. She said she was only going to take a small amount . . . five thousand or so to get us started."

"Would you have gone if you'd known how much she did take? Or if there'd been no money at all?"

I said—"I don't know."—and the words put a thin, humorless smile on Dice's mouth. He knew that was a lie. The "five thousand or so" was the reason I'd let her talk me into going. Just that much was more than I'd ever thought I would get close to in one lump. $85,000 was too much; it scared hell out of me then and still did now.

Dice said: "Tell me the whys, Maguire. I need to know."

"The whys?"

"Why did Fay want to get away from me so badly? Why did she pick a man like you, a parking garage attendant? Why any of it?"

"I don't know why she picked me. I was there, I guess. Available and dumb enough to be willing."

"You weren't her first lover, you know. She had at least three others."

I hadn't known that. But it didn't surprise me; it would have if I'd been the only one.

"But she didn't run away with them," Dice said. "Just you."

"She said she was afraid to stay with you. That's the reason she wanted out."

The words seemed to sting him; he winced and hunched more tightly inside his coat. "Afraid of me? For God's sake, I never harmed or even threatened her. I loved her, Maguire . . . I mean I really loved her. You understand?"

"Yes, sir, I understand."

"I gave her everything she wanted. I treated her like a goddess. What did she have to be afraid of?"

"She let me think you abused her. She didn't tell me the truth until after we quit Chicago."

"Truth?"

"It wasn't you she was scared of . . . it was your clients, the people you work for."

"My God," Dice said.

"She thought you were in too deep. That's what she said. In too deep, and bound to make a mistake someday, and then they'd hurt you. Or her to get back at you."

"She was wrong."

"Well, she didn't think so."

"My practice isn't like that. I've defended men involved in organized crime, yes, but I don't take orders from any of them. I'm still my own man. I'm not in jeopardy and neither was she."

"I'm only telling you what she told me, Mister Dice."

"Why didn't she come to me? Tell me her fears?"

"I don't know. All I know is, she was afraid and that's what started her drinking so much, and all she could think to do was to get out before it was too late, start a new life somewhere else."

"With you and eighty-five thousand dollars from my safe."

"She figured she was entitled to the money," I said. "A settlement, she called it."

"Settlement," he said. Then he said: "What ended it between the two of you in Denver? What she told you about my law practice?"

"Yeah. That, and how much money she'd taken. For all I knew, you'd sent mob enforcers after us. I didn't want any part of that. I still don't."

"So you were the one who wanted out."

"We both wanted out by then. I told her the smart thing was for her to take the money, all of it, and go back to Chicago. No matter how bad she thought things were with you, being on the run by herself would be worse."

"What made you think I'd take her back?"

"She said you loved her, that was one thing she never doubted. You would've taken her back, wouldn't you?"

He didn't answer that. He said: "But she wouldn't listen, is that it? Hard-nosed Fay."

"Not at first. We argued about it for two days straight, both of us drinking too much, before I finally convinced her I was right. We split up the next morning. She took the car and the money and I caught the bus for Salt Lake."

"When did you find out about the accident?"

"Few days later. In one of the Chicago papers I got at a news-stand in Salt Lake."

"She was heading East when it happened. That's what the Nebraska state police told me."

"Yeah. She always drove too fast, even when it was pouring down rain. . . ."

"Rain didn't cause the accident," Dice said. "She was drunk. Three times the legal Nebraska limit."

That was something else that didn't surprise me. But I let it pass without saying anything. The wind gusted; it made a sound in the cranberry stubble like decks of cards being shuffled. There was a funny look on Dice's face, one I couldn't read, and, when he spoke again, it was in a low voice that I could barely hear above the wind.

"Where was she going, Maguire?"

"Where? To Chicago."

"*Was* she coming back to me?" That was the question he'd started to ask earlier; I knew it as soon as I heard it.

"Sure she was."

"What makes you so sure?"

"She told me she was and I believed her."

"Because you'd finally convinced her it was her only option. Because she was even more afraid not to."

"It was more than that," I said. "She still cared for you. She never stopped caring . . . I could see that all along."

"Did she say she still cared?

"Yeah. One of the last things she said before we split up was . . . 'We made a big mistake, Jack. I hope Harry can forgive me. I still care for him, and, if he still loves me after this, maybe the two of us can work something out. It's the only hope I've got left now.'"

He looked at me for a long time, while the wind fluttered around us and one of the other workers fired up a mower. Then his head came up and his shoulders lost their hunch; he seemed to stand taller, like somebody who'd had a heavy weight lifted off him.

I said: "I'm sorry about Fay, Mister Dice. I'm not just saying that . . . I mean it. I'm sorry any of it ever happened."

"All right."

I took a breath before I asked: "So what happens now?"

"Nothing happens. You go back to work and I go back to Chicago."

"And later tonight I get a visitor or two? A bullet in the head? Or just a wheelchair for the rest of my life?"

"You sound like a character in a cheap melodrama."

"Well, what am I supposed to think? You spent three years and plenty of money to track me down. It wasn't so we could have a ten-minute conversation."

"Yes, it was," he said. "So I could ask you the questions you just answered."

"I don't . . . questions?"

"Why Fay left with you. Whether or not she was coming back home when she died. If she still had any love left for me. I had to know, Maguire. You asked me if I'd have taken her back. The answer is yes, in a second. I'd have forgiven her anything, even you, to have her back. I've spent the past three years learning to live without her, but I doubt I could go on many more years without something positive to hang on to." He saw the look on my face and added: "You don't understand, do you?"

"Maybe I do."

"No, because you've never loved a woman the way I loved Fay. But I really don't care if you understand or not. The fact is I don't give any more of a damn about you than I do about the money. I don't hate you, I don't blame you . . . I don't have any feelings at all toward you."

I didn't feel anything, either, right then, not even relief. Later—all that would come later.

His eyes weren't on me any longer. He was staring down into #6 field. "Ironic, isn't it?" he said, and I think it was as much to himself as to me.

"What is?"

"That it should end here, in a place like this. Same kind of place we've been in for three long years, you and me."

"I don't know what you mean, Mister Dice."

"I mean," he said, "we can both stop running now."

And he put his back to me and walked away without looking back.

I quit the fields at five and drove straight to the motel in Ocean Park where I rented a room. I washed up, changed clothes, then lay on the bed and looked at the phone without picking it up. Anne would be home by now and I wanted to talk to her, but I didn't know yet what I would say. It didn't seem right, somehow, to just pretend nothing had changed, that today was the same as yesterday.

I felt the relief now, but nothing much else. No good feelings—just a kind of flatness. Three years. Three years of running, hiding, working at lousy jobs, and living in lonely rooms like this one, and all Harry Dice had wanted was to ask me a few questions. He wasn't a killer or a Mafia big shot on a vendetta; he was a poor sad bastard pining away for a dead love. Well, I'd made it easier for him and for myself in the bargain. I'd told him exactly what he wanted to hear.

The truth, partly. And half truths and outright lies.

Fay hadn't been going back to him when she was killed on that rain-slick highway. She was still running—away from me as well as from him—and, wherever she'd been running to, it hadn't been Chicago. She hadn't had any love left for Harry Dice, if she'd ever loved him in the first place. She'd hated him. That was the real reason she'd run off with me and his money. The last thing she'd said to me was: "I'll never let him find me, Jack, and you better not ever let him find you. I'd die before I'd go back to Chicago. I hate his damn' insides."

I'd had to let her take the car; she threatened to call Dice if I didn't, tell him I'd forced her to go away with me, abused her until she agreed, and she'd run out on me because she was tired of being kicked around. He'd come after me with a vengeance then, she said, kill me himself—and I believed it. When she left, she thought she was taking all the money with her, too. But she was wrong. The two minutes she'd spent in the bathroom before walking out had made her wrong. I'd been afraid she would take it into her head to call Dice anyway, blame everything on me, and I was damned if I would let her get away with leaving me holding an empty bag. I wasn't thinking straight. I hadn't started thinking straight until I got to Salt Lake City.

The $85,000 hadn't burned up in the car smash; it had been with me on the bus, 200 miles away. Almost the entire amount was in a bank in Seattle right now, earning interest, and had been even before I found out Fay was dead.

Three years, and all I'd spent of it was a few hundred dollars. I'd been afraid to spend more. Afraid Dice would hunt even harder if he thought I was living it up on his money. Afraid to send it back to him because what if I really needed it someday, to leave the country? Afraid all the time, afraid of everything.

But now I didn't have to be afraid. Dice really didn't care about the money; he'd had no reason to lie to me about that. It was all mine and I could do what I wanted with it. Spend it on Anne—except that Anne had no interest in money or what it could buy. And I couldn't think of anything I wanted to buy for myself, either. Not a single thing.

That was the reason for the flat feeling. Admit it, Maguire. Dice didn't care about the money, Anne wouldn't care, and after three years you don't care, either.

In my mind I could see Dice, standing on the levee road, staring down into the cranberry field. And I could hear him saying: *Ironic, isn't it? . . . That it should end here, in a place like this. Same kind of place we've been in for three long years, you and me.* I hadn't known then what he meant, but I knew now. Bogs. The two of us like men running in a swamp, weighted down with baggage, and going nowhere, and, if we'd kept up the chase much longer, we'd have been mired so deep we'd never have gotten out.

The money and the fear were my baggage, just like Dice's

love for Fay had been his. I'd gotten rid of the fear—and I could get rid of the money, too. Anne's charity work. $85,000 plus interest would do a lot of needy people a lot of good. I could tell her I'd inherited it . . . no. No. Tell her the truth, the whole story. No more lies, especially not to Anne. No more baggage.

I sat up and reached for the phone. The flatness was gone; now I had the good feeling I'd been waiting for all day. I didn't have to leave Anne or Long Beach. Dice had been right. We could both stop running. And I could start living again.

His Name Was Legion

His name was Legion.

No, sir, I mean that literal—Jimmy Legion, that was his name. He knew about the Biblical connection, though. Used to say— "My name is Legion."—like he was Christ Himself quoting Scripture.

Religious man? No, sir! Furthest thing from it. Jimmy Legion was a liar, a blasphemer, a thief, a fornicator, and just about anything else you can name. A pure hellion—a devil's son if ever there was one. Some folks in Wayville said that after he ran off with Amanda Sykes that September of 1931, he sure must have crossed afoul of the law and come to a violent end. But nobody rightly knew for sure. Not about him, nor about Amanda Sykes, either.

He came to Wayville in the summer of that year, 1931. Came in out of nowhere in a fancy new Ford car, seemed to have plenty of money in his pockets, claimed he was a magazine writer. Wayville wasn't much in those days—just a small farm town with a population of around 500. Hardly the kind of place you'd expect a man like Legion to gravitate to. Unless he was hiding out from the law right then, which is the way some folks figured it—but only after he was gone. While he lived in Wayville, he was a charmer.

First day I laid eyes on him, I was riding out from town with saddlebags and a pack all loaded up with small hardware. Yes, that's right—saddlebags. I was only nineteen that summer, and my family was too poor to afford an automobile. But my father gave me a horse of my own when I was sixteen—a fine light-colored gelding that I called Silverboy—and after I was graduated from high school I went to work for Mr. Hazlitt at Wayville Hardware.

Depression had hit everybody pretty hard in our area, and not many small farmers could afford the gasoline for truck trips into town every time they needed something. Small merchants like Mr. Hazlitt couldn't afford it, either. So what I did for him, I used Silverboy to deliver small things like farm tools and plumbing supplies and carpentry items. Rode him most of the time, hitched him to a wagon once in a while when the load was too large to carry on horseback. Mr. Hazlitt called me Ben Boone the Pony Express Deliveryman, and I liked that fine. I was full of spirit and adventure back then.

Anyhow, this afternoon I'm talking about I was riding Silverboy out to the Baker farm when I heard a roar on the road behind me. Then a car shot by so fast and so close that Silverboy spooked and spilled both of us down a ten-foot embankment.

Wasn't either of us hurt, but we could have been—we could have been killed. I only got a glimpse of the car, but it was enough for me to identify it when I got back to Wayville. I went hunting for the owner and found him straightaway inside Chancellor's Café.

First thing he said to me was: "My name is Legion."

Well, we had words. Or rather, I had the words; he just stood there and grinned at me, all wise and superior, like a professor talking to a bumpkin. Handsome brute, he was, few years older than me, with slicked-down hair and big brown eyes and teeth so white they glistened like mica rocks in the sun.

He shamed me, is what he did, in front of a dozen of my friends and neighbors. Said what happened on the road was my fault, and why didn't I go somewhere and curry my horse, he had better things to do than argue road right of ways.

Every time I saw him after that he'd make some remark to me. Polite, but with brimstone in it—I guess you know what I mean. I tried to fight him once, but he wouldn't fight. Just stood grinning at me like the first time, hands down at his sides, daring me. I couldn't hit him that way, when he wouldn't defend himself. I wanted to, but I was raised better than that.

If me and some of the other young fellows disliked him, most of the girls took to him like flies to honey. All they saw were his smile and his big brown eyes and his city charm. And his lies about being a magazine writer.

Just about every day I'd see him with a different girl, some I'd dated myself on occasion, such as Bobbie Jones and Dulcea Wade. Oh, he was smooth and evil, all right. He ruined more than one those girls, no doubt of that. Got Dulcea Wade pregnant, for one, although none of us found out about it until after he ran off with Amanda Sykes.

Falsehoods and fornication were only two of his sins. Like I said before, he was guilty of much more than that. Including plain thievery.

He wasn't in town more than a month before folks started missing things. Small amounts of cash money, valuables of one kind or another. Mrs. Cooley, who owned the boarding house where Legion took a room, lost a solid gold ring her late husband gave her. But she never suspected Legion, and hardly anybody else did, either, until it was too late.

All this went on for close to three months—the lying and the fornicating and the stealing. It couldn't have lasted much longer than that without the truth coming out, and I guess Legion knew that best of all. It was a Friday in late September that he and Amanda Sykes disappeared together. And when folks did learn the truth about him, all they could say was good riddance to him and her both—the Sykeses among them because they were decent God-fearing people.

I reckon I was one of the last to see either of them. Fact is, in a way I was responsible for them leaving as sudden as they did. At about two o'clock that Friday afternoon I left Mr. Hazlitt's store with a scythe and some other tools George Pickett needed on his farm and rode out the north road. It was a burning hot day, no wind at all—I remember that clear. When I was two miles outside Wayville, and about two more from the Pickett farm, I took Silverboy over to a stream that meandered through a stand of cottonwoods. He was blowing pretty hard because of the heat, and I wanted to give him a cool drink. Give myself a cool drink, too.

But no sooner did I rein him up to the stream than I spied two people lying together in the tall grass. And I mean "lying together" in the Biblical sense—no need to explain further. It was Legion and Amanda Sykes.

Well, they were so involved in their sinning that they didn't notice me until I was right up to them. Before I could turn Silverboy and set him running, Legion jumped up and grabbed hold of me and dragged me down to the ground. He cursed me like a crazy man; I never saw anybody that wild and possessed before or since.

"I'll teach you to spy on me, Ben Boone!" he shouted, and he hit me a full right-hand wallop on the face. Knocked me down in the grass and bloodied my nose, bloodied it so bad I couldn't stop the flow until a long while later.

Then he jumped on me and pounded me two more blows until I was half senseless. And after that he reached in my pocket and took my wallet—stole my wallet and all the money I had.

Amanda Sykes just sat there covering herself with her dress and watching. She never said a word the whole time.

It wasn't a minute later they were gone. I saw them get into his Ford that was hidden in the cottonwoods nearby and roar away. I couldn't have stopped them with a rifle, weak as I was.

When my strength finally came back, I washed the blood off me as best I could, and rode Silverboy straight back to Wayville to report to the local constable. He called in the state police and they put out a warrant for the arrest of Legion and Amanda Sykes, but nothing came of it. Police didn't find them; nobody ever heard of them again.

Yes, sir, I know the story doesn't seem to have much point right now. But it will in just a minute. I wanted you to hear it first the way I told it back in 1931—the way I been telling it over and over in my own mind ever since then so I could keep on living with myself.

A good part of it's lies, you see. Lies worse than Jimmy Legion's.

That's why I asked you to come, Reverend. Doctors here at the hospital tell me my heart's about ready to give out. They don't figure I'll last the week. I can't die with sin on my soul. Time's long past due for me to make peace with myself and with God.

The lies? Mostly what happened on that last afternoon, after I came riding up to the stream on my way to the Pickett farm. About Legion attacking me and bloodying me and stealing my wallet. About him and Amanda Sykes running off together. About not telling of the sinkhole near the stream that was big enough and deep enough to swallow anything smaller than a house.

Those things, and the names of two of the three of us that were there.

No, I didn't mean him. Everything I told you about him is the truth as far as I know it, including his name.

His name was Legion.

But Amanda's name wasn't Sykes. Not any more it wasn't,

not for five months prior to that day. Her name was Amanda Boone.

Yes, Reverend, that's right—she was my wife. I'd dated those other girls, but I'd long courted Amanda; we eloped over the state line before Legion arrived and got married by a justice of the peace. We did it that way because her folks and mine were dead set against either of us marrying so young—not that they knew we were at such a stage. We kept that part of our relationship a secret, too, I guess, because it was an adventure for the both of us, at least in the beginning.

My name? Yes, it's really Ben Boone. Yet it wasn't on that afternoon. The one who chanced on Legion and Amanda out there by the stream, who caught them sinning and listened to them laugh all shameless and say they were running off together . . . he wasn't Ben Boone at all.

His name, Reverend, that one who sat grim on his pale horse with Farmer Pickett's long, new-honed scythe in one hand . . . his name was Death.

THE ARROWMONT PRISON RIDDLE

I first met the man who called himself by the unlikely name of Buckmaster Gilloon in the late summer of 1916, my second year as warden of Arrowmont Prison. There were no living quarters within the old brick walls of the prison, which was situated on a promontory overlooking a small winding river two miles north of Arrowmont Village, so I had rented a cottage in the village proper, not far from a tavern known as Hallahan's Irish Inn. It was in this tavern, and as a result of a mutual passion for Guinness stout and the game of darts, that Gilloon and I became acquainted.

As a man he was every bit as unlikely as his name. He was in his late thirties, short, and almost painfully thin; he had a glass eye and a drooping and incongruous Oriental-style mustache, wore English tweeds, gaudy Albert watch chains and plaid Scotch caps, and always carried half a dozen loose-leaf notebooks in which he perpetually and secretively jotted things. He was well read and erudite, had a repertoire of bawdy stories to rival any vaudevillian in the country, and never seemed to lack ready cash. He lived in a boarding house in the center of the village and claimed to be a writer for the pulp magazines— *Argosy, Adventure, All-Story Weekly, Munsey's.* Perhaps he was, but he steadfastly refused to discuss any of his fiction, or to divulge his pseudonym or pseudonyms.

He was reticent about divulging any personal information. When personal questions arose, he deftly changed the subject.

Since he did not speak with an accent, I took him to be American born. I was able to learn, from occasional comments and observations, that he had traveled extensively throughout the world.

In my nine decades on this earth I have never encountered a more fascinating or troubling enigma than this man whose path crossed mine for a few short weeks in 1916.

Who and what was Buckmaster Gilloon? Is it possible for one enigma to be attracted and motivated by another enigma? Can that which seems natural and coincidental be the result instead of preternatural forces? These questions have plagued me in the sixty years since Gilloon and I became involved in what appeared to be an utterly enigmatic crime.

It all began on September 26, 1916—the day of the scheduled execution at Arrowmont Prison of a condemned murderer named Arthur Teasdale. . . .

Shortly before noon of that day a thunderstorm struck without warning. Rain pelted down from a black sky, and lightning crackled in low jagged blazes that gave the illusion of striking unseen objects just beyond the prison walls. I was already suffering from nervous tension, as was always the case on the day of an execution, and the storm added to my discomfort. I passed the early afternoon sitting at my desk, staring out the window, listening to the inexorable *ticking* of my Seth Thomas, wishing the execution was done with and it was eight o'clock, when I was due to meet Gilloon at Hallahan's for Guinness and darts.

At 3:30 the two civilians who had volunteered to act as witnesses to the hanging arrived. I ushered them into a waiting room and asked them to wait until they were summoned. Then I donned a slicker and stopped by the office of Rogers, the chief guard, and asked him to accompany me to the execution shed.

The shed was relatively small, constructed of brick with a tin roof, and sat in a corner of the prison between the textile mill and the iron foundry. It was lighted by lanterns hung from the walls and the rafters and contained only a row of witness chairs and a high permanent gallows at the far end. Attached to the shed's north wall was an annex in which the death cell was located. As was customary, Teasdale had been transported there five days earlier to await due process.

He was a particularly vicious and evil man, Teasdale. He had cold-bloodedly murdered three people during an abortive robbery attempt in the state capital, and had been anything but a model prisoner during his month's confinement at Arrowmont. As a rule I had a certain compassion for those condemned to hang under my jurisdiction, and in two cases I had spoken to the governor in favor of clemency. In Teasdale's case, however, I had conceded that a continuance of his life would serve no good purpose.

When I had visited him the previous night to ask if he wished to see a clergyman or to order anything special for his last meal, he had cursed me and Rogers and the entire prison personnel with an almost maniacal intensity, vowing vengeance on us all from the grave.

I rather expected, as Rogers and I entered the death cell at ten minutes of four, to find Teasdale in much the same state. However, he had fallen instead into an acute melancholia; he lay on his cot with his knees drawn up and his eyes staring blankly at the opposite wall. The two guards assigned to him, Hollowell and Granger (Granger was also the state-appointed hangman), told us he had been like that for several hours. I spoke to him, asking again if he wished to confer with a clergyman. He did not answer, did not move. I inquired if he had any last requests, and if it was his wish to wear a hood for his final walk to the gallows and for the execution. He did not respond.

I took Hollowell aside. "Perhaps it would be better to use the hood," I said. "It will make it easier for all of us."

"Yes, sir."

Rogers and I left the annex, accompanied by Granger, for a final examination of the gallows. The rope had already been hung and the hangman's knot tied. While Granger made certain they were secure, I unlocked the door beneath the platform, which opened into a short passage that ended in a narrow cubicle beneath the trap. The platform had been built eight feet off the floor, so that the death throes of the condemned man would be concealed from the witnesses—a humane gesture which was not observed by all prisons in our state, and for which I was grateful.

After I had made a routine examination of the cubicle, and re-locked the door, I mounted the thirteen steps to the platform. The trap beneath the gibbet arm was operated by a lever set into the floor; when Granger threw the lever, the trap would fall open. Once we tried it and reset it, I pronounced everything in readiness and sent Rogers to summon the civilian witnesses and the prison doctor. It was then 4:35 and the execution would take place at precisely five o'clock. I had received a wire from the governor the night before, informing me that there wasn't the remotest chance of a stay being granted.

When Rogers returned with the witnesses and the doctor, we all took chairs in the row arranged some forty feet opposite the gallows. Time passed tensely, with thunder echoing outside, a hard rain drumming against the tin roof, and eerie shadows not entirely dispelled by the lantern light; the moments before that execution were particularly disquieting.

I held my pocket watch open on my knee, and at 4:55 I signaled to the guard at the annex door to call for the prisoner. Three more minutes crept by, and then the door reopened and Granger and Hollowell brought Teasdale into the shed.

The three men made a grim procession as they crossed to the

gallows steps—Granger in his black hangman's duster, Hollowell in his khaki guard uniform and peaked cap, Teasdale between them in his gray prison clothing and black hood. Teasdale's shoes dragged across the floor—he was a stiffly unresisting weight until they reached the steps, then he struggled briefly, and Granger and Hollowell were forced to tighten their grip and all but carry him up onto the gallows. Hollowell held him slumped on the trap while Granger solemnly fitted the noose around his neck and drew it taut.

The hands on my watch read five o'clock when, as prescribed by law, Granger intoned: "Have you any last words before the sentence imposed on you is carried out?"

Teasdale said nothing, but his body twisted with a spasm of fear.

Granger looked in my direction and I raised my hand to indicate final sanction. He backed away from Teasdale and rested his hand on the release lever. As he did so, there came from outside a long, rolling peal of thunder that seemed to shake the shed roof. A chill touched the nape of my neck and I shifted uneasily on my chair.

Just as the sound of the thunder faded, Granger threw the lever and Hollowell released Teasdale and stepped back. The trap *thudded* open and the condemned man plummeted downward.

In that same instant I thought I saw a faint silvery glimmer above the opening, but it was so brief that I took it for an optical illusion. My attention was focused on the rope: it danced for a moment under the weight of the body, then pulled taut and became motionless. I let out a soft tired sigh and sat forward while Granger and Hollowell, both of whom were looking away from the open trap, silently counted off the passage of sixty seconds.

When the minute had elapsed, Granger turned and walked to

the edge of the trap. If the body hung laxly, he would signal to me so that the prison doctor and I could enter the cubicle and officially pronounce Teasdale deceased; if the body was still thrashing, thus indicating the condemned man's neck had not been broken in the fall—grisly prospect, but I had seen it happen—more time would be allowed to pass. It sounds brutal, I know, but such was the law and it had to be obeyed without question.

But Granger's reaction was so peculiar and so violent that I came immediately to my feet. He flinched as if he had been struck in the stomach and his face twisted into an expression of disbelief. He dropped to his hands and knees at the front of the trap as Hollowell came up beside him and leaned down to peer into the passageway.

"What is it, Granger?" I called. "What's the matter?"

He straightened after a few seconds and pivoted toward me. "You better get up here, Warden Parker," he said. His voice was shrill and tremulous and he clutched at his stomach. "Quick!"

Rogers and I exchanged glances, then ran to the steps, mounted them, and hurried to the trap, the other guards and the prison doctor close behind us. As soon as I looked downward, it was my turn to stare with incredulity, to exclaim against what I saw—and what I did not see.

The hangman's noose at the end of the rope was empty. Except for the black hood on the ground, the cubicle was empty. Impossibly the body of Arthur Teasdale had vanished.

I raced down the gallows steps and fumbled the platform door open with my key. I had the vague desperate hope that Teasdale had somehow slipped the noose and that I would see him lying within, against the door—that small section of the passageway was shrouded in darkness and not quite penetrable from above—but he wasn't there. The passageway, like the cubicle, was deserted.

While I called for a lantern, Rogers hoisted up the rope to examine it and the noose. A moment later he announced that it had not been tampered with in any way. When a guard brought the lantern, I embarked on a careful search of the area, but there were no loose boards in the walls of the passage or the cubicle, and the floor was of solid concrete. On the floor I discovered a thin sliver of wood about an inch long, which may or may not have been there previously. Aside from that, there was not so much as a strand of hair or a loose thread to be found. And the black hood told me nothing at all.

There simply did not seem to be any way Teasdale—or his remains—could have gotten, or been gotten, out of there.

I stood for a moment, staring at the flickering light from the lantern, listening to the distant rumbling of thunder. Had Teasdale died at the end of the hangman's rope? Or had he somehow managed to cheat death? I had seen him fall through the trap with my own eyes, had seen the rope dance, and then pull taut with the weight of his body. He must have expired, I told myself.

A shiver moved along my back. I found myself remembering Teasdale's threats to wreak vengeance from the grave, and I had the irrational thought that perhaps something otherworldly had been responsible for the phenomenon we had witnessed. Teasdale had, after all, been a malignant individual. Could he have been so evil that he had managed to summon the powers of darkness to save him in the instant before death—or to claim him soul and body in the instant after it?

I refused to believe it. I am a practical man, not prone to superstition, and it has always been my nature to seek a logical explanation for even the most uncommon occurrence. Arthur Teasdale had disappeared, yes, but it could not be other than an earthly force behind the deed. Which meant that, alive or dead, Teasdale was still somewhere inside the walls of Arrowmont Prison.

I roused myself, left the passageway, and issued instructions for a thorough search of the prison grounds. I ordered word sent to the guards in the watchtowers to double their normal vigilance. I noticed that Hollowell wasn't present along with the assembled guards and asked where he had gone. One of the others said he had seen Hollowell hurry out of the shed several minutes earlier.

Frowning, I pondered this information. Had Hollowell intuited something, or even seen something, and gone off unwisely to investigate on his own rather than confide in the rest of us? He had been employed at Arrowmont Prison less than two months, so I knew relatively little about him. I requested that he be found and brought to my office.

When Rogers and Granger and the other guards had departed, I escorted the two civilian witnesses to the administration building, where I asked them to remain until the mystery was explained. As I settled grimly at my desk to await Hollowell and word on the search of the grounds, I expected such an explanation within the hour.

I could not, however, have been more wrong.

The first development came after thirty minutes, and it was nearly as alarming as the disappearance of Teasdale from the gallows cubicle. One of the guards brought the news that a body had been discovered behind a stack of lumber in a lean-to between the execution shed and the iron foundry. But it was not the body of Arthur Teasdale.

It was that of Hollowell, stabbed to death with an awl.

I went immediately. As I stood beneath the rain-swept lean-to, looking down at the bloody front of poor Hollowell's uniform, a fresh set of unsettling questions tumbled through my mind. Had he been killed because, as I had first thought, he had either seen or intuited something connected with Teasdale's disappearance? If that was the case, whatever it was had died with him.

Or was it possible that he had himself been involved in the disappearance and been murdered to assure his silence? But how could he have been involved? He had been in my sight the entire time on the gallows platform. He had done nothing suspicious, could not in any way I could conceive have assisted in the deed.

How could Teasdale have survived the hanging? How could he have escaped not only the gallows but the execution shed itself?

The only explanation seemed to be that it was not a live Arthur Teasdale who was carrying out his warped revenge, but a dead one who had been embraced and given earthly powers by the forces of evil. . . .

In order to dispel the dark reflections from my mind, I personally supervised the balance of the search. Tines of lightning split the sky and thunder continued to hammer the roofs as we went from building to building. No corner of the prison compound escaped our scrutiny. No potential hiding place was overlooked. We went so far as to test for the presence of tunnels in the work areas and in the individual cells, although I had instructed just such a search only weeks before as part of my security program.

We found nothing.

Alive or dead, Arthur Teasdale was no longer within the walls of Arrowmont Prison.

I left the prison at ten o'clock that night. There was nothing more to be done, and I was filled with such depression and anxiety that I could not bear to spend another minute there. I had debated contacting the governor, of course, and, wisely or not, had decided against it for the time being. He would think me a lunatic if I requested assistance in a county or statewide search for a man who had for all intents and purposes been hanged at five o'clock that afternoon. If there were no new developments within the next twenty-four hours, I knew I would have no choice but to explain the situation to him. And I had no doubt that such an explanation unaccompanied by Teasdale or Teasdale's remains would cost me my position.

Before leaving, I swore everyone to secrecy, saying that I would have any man's job if he leaked word of the day's events to the press or to the public at large. The last thing I wanted was rumor-mongering and a general panic as a result of it. I warned Granger and the other guards who had come in contact with Teasdale to be especially wary and left word that I was to be contacted immediately if there were any further developments before morning.

I had up to that time given little thought to my own safety. But when I reached my cottage in the village, I found myself imagining menace in every shadow and sound. Relaxation was impossible. After twenty minutes I felt impelled to leave, to seek out a friendly face. I told my housekeeper I would be at Hallahan's Irish Inn if anyone called for me and drove my Packard to the tavern.

The first person I saw upon entering was Buckmaster Gilloon. He was seated alone in a corner booth, writing in one of his notebooks, a stein of draft Guinness at his elbow.

Gilloon had always been very secretive about his notebooks and never allowed anyone to glimpse so much as a word of what he put into them. But he was so engrossed when I walked up to the booth that he did not hear me, and I happened to glance down at the open page on which he was writing. There was but a single interrogative sentence on the page, clearly legible in his bold hand. The sentence read:

If a jimbuck stands alone by the sea, on a night when the dark moon sings, how many grains of sand in a single one of his foot prints?

That sentence has always haunted me, because I cannot begin to understand its significance. I have no idea what a "jimbuck" is, except perhaps as a fictional creation, and yet that passage was like none that ever appeared in such periodicals as *Argosy* or *Munsey's*.

Gilloon sensed my presence after a second or two, and he slammed the notebook shut. A ferocious scowl crossed his normally placid features. He said irritably: "Reading over a man's shoulder is a nasty habit, Parker."

"I'm sorry, I didn't mean to pry. . . ."

"I'll thank you to be more respectful of my privacy in the future."

"Yes, of course." I sank wearily into the booth opposite him and called for a Guinness.

Gilloon studied me across the table. "You look haggard, Parker. What's troubling you?"

"It's . . . nothing."

"Everything is something."

"I'm not at liberty to discuss it."

"Would it have anything to do with the execution at Arrowmont Prison this afternoon?"

I blinked. "Why would you surmise that?"

"Logical assumption," Gilloon said. "You are obviously upset, and yet you are a man who lives quietly and suffers no apparent personal problems. You are warden of Arrowmont Prison and the fact of the execution is public knowledge. You customarily come to the inn at eight o'clock, and yet you didn't make your appearance tonight until after eleven."

I said: "I wish I had your mathematical mind, Gilloon."

"Indeed? Why is that?"

"Perhaps then I could find answers where none seem to exist."

"Answers to what?"

A waiter arrived with my Guinness and I took a swallow gratefully.

Gilloon was looking at me with piercing interest. I avoided his one-eyed gaze, knowing I had already said too much. But there was something about Gilloon that demanded confidence. Perhaps he could shed some light on the riddle of Teasdale's disappearance.

"Come now, Parker . . . answers to what?" he repeated. "Has something happened at the prison?"

And, of course, I weakened—partly because of frustration and worry, partly because the possibility that I might never learn the secret loomed large and painful. "Yes," I said, "something has happened at the prison. Something incredible, and I mean that literally." I paused to draw a heavy breath. "If I tell you about it, do I have your word that you won't let it go beyond this table?"

"Naturally." Gilloon leaned forward and his good eye glittered with anticipation. "Go on, Parker."

More or less calmly at first, then with increasing agitation as I relived the events, I proceeded to tell Gilloon everything that had transpired at the prison. He listened with attention, not once interrupting. I had never seen him excited prior to that night, but, when I had finished, he was fairly squirming. He took off his Scotch cap and ran a hand through his thinning brown hair.

"Fascinating tale," he said.

"Horrifying would be a more appropriate word."

"That, too, yes. No wonder you're upset."

"It defies explanation," I said. "And yet there has to be one. I refuse to accept the supernatural implications."

"I wouldn't be so skeptical of the supernatural if I were you, Parker. I've come across a number of things in my travels which could not be satisfactorily explained by man or science."

I stared at him. "Does that mean you believe Teasdale's disappearance was arranged by forces beyond human ken?"

"No, no. I was merely making a considered observation. Have you given me every detail of what happened?"

"I believe so."

"Think it through again . . . be sure."

Frowning, I reviewed the events once more. And it came to me that I had neglected to mention the brief silvery glimmer which had appeared above the trap in the instant Teasdale plunged through; I had, in fact, forgotten all about it. This time I mentioned it to Gilloon.

"Ah," he said.

"Ah? Does it have significance?"

"Perhaps. Can you be more specific about it?"

"I'm afraid not. It was so brief I took it at the time for an optical illusion."

"You saw no other such glimmers?"

"None."

"How far away from the gallows were you sitting?"

"Approximately forty feet."

"Is the shed equipped with electric lights?"

"No . . . lanterns."

"I see," Gilloon said meditatively. He seized one of his notebooks, opened it, shielded it from my eyes with his left arm, and began to write with his pencil. He wrote without pause for a good three minutes, until I grew both irritated and anxious.

"Gilloon," I said, "stop that infernal scribbling and tell me what's on your mind."

He gave no indication of having heard me. His pencil continued to scratch against the paper, filling another page.

Except for the movement of his right hand and one side of his mouth gnawing at the edge of his mustache, he was as rigid as a block of stone.

"Damn it, Gilloon!"

But it was another ten seconds before the pencil became motionless. He stared at what he had written, and then looked up at me. "Parker," he said, "did Arthur Teasdale have a trade?"

The question took me by surprise. "A trade?"

"Yes. What did he do for a living, if anything?"

"What bearing can that have on what's happened?"

"Perhaps a great deal," Gilloon said.

"He worked in a textile mill."

"And there is a textile mill at the prison, correct?"

"Yes."

"Does it stock quantities of silk?"

"Silk? Yes, on occasion. What . . . ?"

I did not finish what I was about to say, for he had shut me out and resumed writing in his notebook. I repressed an oath of exasperation, took a long draft of Guinness to calm myself, and prepared to demand that he tell me what theory he had devised. Before I could do that, however, Gilloon abruptly closed the notebook, slid out of the booth, and loomed over me.

"I'll need to see the execution shed," he said.

"What for?"

"Corroboration of certain facts."

"But. . . ." I stood up hastily. "You've suspicioned a possible answer, that's clear, though I can't for the life of me see how, on the basis of the information I've given you. What is it?"

"I must see the execution shed," he said firmly. "I will not voice premature speculations."

It touched my mind that the man was a bit mad. After all, I had only known him for a few weeks, and from the first he had been decidedly eccentric in most respects. Still, I had never had cause to question his mental faculties before this, and the aura of self-assurance and confidence he projected was forceful. Because I was so desperate to solve the riddle, I couldn't afford not to indulge, at least for a while, the one man who might be able to provide it.

"Very well," I said, "I'll take you to the prison."

Rain still fell in black torrents—although without thunder and lightning—when I brought my Packard around the last climbing curve onto the promontory. Lantern light glowed fuzzily in the prison watchtowers, and the bare brick walls had an unpleasant oily sheen. At this hour of night, in the storm, the place seemed forbidding and shrouded in human despair—an atmosphere I had not previously apprehended during the two years I had been its warden. Strange how a brush with the unknown can alter one's perspective and stir the fears that lie at the bottom of one's soul.

Beside me Gilloon did not speak; he sat erect, his hands resting on the notebooks on his lap. I parked in the small lot facing the main gates, and, after Gilloon had carefully tucked the notebooks inside his slicker, we ran through the downpour to the gates. I gestured to the guard, who nodded beneath the hood of his oilskin, allowed us to enter, and then quickly closed the iron halves behind us and returned to the warmth of the gatehouse. I led Gilloon directly across the compound to the execution shed.

The guards I had posted inside seemed edgy and grateful for company. It was colder now, and, despite the fact that all the lanterns were lit, it also seemed darker and filled with more restless shadows. But the earlier aura of spiritual menace permeated the air, at least to my sensitivities. If Gilloon noticed it, he gave no indication.

He wasted no time crossing to the gallows and climbing the

steps to the platform. I followed him to the trap, which still hung open. Gilloon peered into the cubicle, got onto all fours to squint in the rectangular edges of the opening, and then hoisted the hangman's rope and studied the noose. Finally, with surprising agility, he dropped down inside the cubicle, requesting a lantern that I fetched for him, and spent minutes crawling about with his nose to the floor. He located the thin splinter of wood I had noticed earlier, studied it in the lantern glow, and dropped it into the pocket of his tweed coat.

When he came out through the passageway, he wore a look mixed of ferocity and satisfaction. "Stand there a minute, will you?" he said. He hurried over to where the witness chairs were arranged, then called: "In which of these chairs were you sitting during the execution?"

"Fourth one from the left."

Gilloon sat in that chair, produced his notebooks, opened one, and bent over it. I waited with mounting agitation while he committed notes to paper. When he glanced up again, the flickering lantern glow gave his face a spectral cast.

He said: "While Granger placed the noose over Teasdale's head, Hollowell held the prisoner on the trap . . . is that correct?"

"It is."

"Stand as Hollowell was standing."

I moved to the edge of the opening, turning slightly quarter profile.

"You're certain that was the exact position?"

"Yes."

"Once the trap had been sprung, what did Hollowell do?"

"Moved a few paces away." I demonstrated.

"Did he avert his eyes from the trap?"

"Yes, he did. So did Granger. That's standard procedure."

"Which direction did he face?"

145

I frowned. "I'm not quite sure. My attention was on the trap and the rope."

"You're doing admirably, Parker. After Granger threw the trap lever, did he remain standing beside it?"

"Until he had counted off sixty seconds, yes."

"And then?"

"As I told you, he walked to the trap and looked into the cubicle. Again, that is standard procedure for the hangman. When he saw it was empty, he uttered a shocked exclamation, went to his knees, and leaned down to see if Teasdale had somehow slipped the noose and fallen or crawled into the passageway."

"At which part of the opening did he go to his knees? Front, rear, one of the sides?"

"The front. But I don't see. . . ."

"Would you mind illustrating?"

I grumbled but did as he asked. Some thirty seconds passed in silence. Finally I stood and turned, and, of course, found Gilloon again writing in his notebook. I descended the gallows steps. Gilloon closed the notebook and stood with an air of growing urgency. "Where would Granger be at this hour?" he asked. "Still here at the prison?"

"I doubt it. He came on duty at three and should have gone off again at midnight."

"It's imperative that we find him as soon as possible, Parker. Now that I'm onto the solution of this riddle, there's no time to waste."

"You have solved it?"

"I'm certain I have." He hurried out of the shed.

I felt dazed as we crossed the rain-soaked compound, yet Gilloon's positiveness had infused in me a similar sense of urgency. We entered the administration building and I led the way to Rogers's office, where we found him preparing to depart for the night. When I asked about Granger, Rogers said that he had signed out some fifty minutes earlier, at midnight.

"Where does he live?" Gilloon asked us.

"In Hainesville, I think."

"We must go there immediately, Parker. And we had better take half a dozen well-armed men with us."

"Do you honestly believe that's necessary?"

"I do," Gilloon said. "If we're fortunate, it will help prevent another murder."

The six-mile drive to the village of Hainesville was charged with tension, made even more acute by the muddy roads and the pelting rain. Gilloon stubbornly refused to comment on the way as to whether he believed Granger to be a culpable or innocent party, or as to whether he expected to find Arthur Teasdale alive—or dead—at Granger's home. There would be time enough later for explanations, he said.

Hunched over the wheel of the Packard, conscious of the two heavily armed prison guards in the rear seat and the headlamps of Rogers's car following closely behind, I could not help but wonder if I might be making a prize fool of myself. Suppose I had been wrong in my judgment of Gilloon, and he was daft after all? Or a well-meaning fool in his own right? Or worst of all, a hoaxster?

Nevertheless, there was no turning back now. I had long since committed myself. Whatever the outcome, I had placed the fate of my career firmly in the hands of Buckmaster Gilloon.

We entered the outskirts of Hainesville. One of the guards who rode with us lived there, and he directed us down the main street and into a turn just beyond the church. The lane in which Granger lived, he said, was two blocks farther up and one block east.

Beside me Gilloon spoke for the first time. "I suggest we park a distance away from Granger's residence, Parker. It won't do to announce our arrival by stopping in front."

I nodded. When I made the turn into the lane, I took the Packard onto the verge and doused its lights. Rogers's car drifted in behind, headlamps also winking out. A moment later eight of us stood in a tight group in the roadway, huddling inside our slickers as we peered up the lane.

There were four houses in the block, two on each side, spaced widely apart. The pair on our left, behind which stretched open meadow land, were dark. The farthest of the two on the right was also dark, but the closer one showed light in one of the front windows. Thick smoke curled out of its chimney and was swirled into nothingness by the howling wind. A huge oak shaded the front yard. Across the rear, a copse of swaying pine stood silhouetted against the black sky.

The guard who lived in Hainesville said: "That's Granger's place, the one showing light."

We left the road and set out across the grassy flatland to the pines, then through them toward Granger's cottage. From a point behind the house, after issuing instructions for the others to wait there, Gilloon, Rogers, and I made our way downward past an old stone well and through a sodden growth of weeds. The sound of the storm muffled our approach as we proceeded single file, Gilloon tacitly assuming leadership, along the west side of the house to the lighted window.

Gilloon put his head around the frame for the first cautious look inside. Momentarily he stepped back and motioned me to take his place. When I had moved to where I could peer in, I saw Granger standing relaxed before the fireplace, using a poker to prod a blazing fire not wholly composed of logs—something else, a blackened lump already burned beyond recognition, was being consumed there. But he was not alone in the room; a second man stood watching him, an old hammerless revolver tucked into the waistband of his trousers.

Arthur Teasdale.

I experienced a mixture of relief, rage, and resolve as I moved away to give Rogers his turn. It was obvious that Granger was guilty of complicity in Teasdale's escape—and I had always liked and trusted the man. But I supposed everyone had his price; I may even have had a fleeting wonder as to what my own might be.

After Rogers had his look, the three of us returned to the back yard, where I told him to prepare the rest of the men for a front and rear assault on the cottage. Then Gilloon and I took up post in the shadows behind the stone well. Now that my faith in him had been vindicated, I felt an enormous gratitude—but this was hardly the time to express it. Or to ask any of the questions that were racing through my mind. We waited in silence.

In less than four minutes all six of my men had surrounded the house. I could not hear it when those at the front broke in, but the men at the back entered the rear door swiftly. Soon the sound of pistol shots rose above the cry of the storm.

Gilloon and I hastened inside. In the parlor we found Granger sitting on the floor beside the hearth, his head buried in his hands. He had not been injured, nor had any of the guards. Teasdale was lying just beyond the entrance to the center hallway. The front of his shirt was bloody, but he had merely suffered a superficial shoulder wound and was cursing like a madman. He would live to hang again, I remember thinking, in the execution shed at Arrowmont Prison.

Sixty minutes later, after Teasdale had been placed under heavy guard in the prison infirmary and a silent Granger had been locked in a cell, Rogers and Gilloon and I met in my office. Outside, the rain had slackened to a drizzle.

"Now then, Gilloon," I began, "we owe you a great debt, and I acknowledge it here and now. But explanations are long overdue."

He smiled with the air of a man who has just been through an exhilarating experience. "Of course," he said. "Suppose we begin with Hollowell. You're wondering if he was bribed by Teasdale . . . if he also assisted in the escape. The answer is no. He was an innocent pawn."

"Then why was he killed? Revenge?"

"Not at all. His life was taken . . . and not at the place where his body was later discovered . . . so that the escape trick could be worked in the first place. It was one of the primary keys to the plan's success."

"I don't understand," I said. "The escape trick had already been completed when Hollowell was stabbed."

"Ah, but it hadn't," Galloon said. "Hollowell was murdered before the execution, sometime between four and five o'clock."

We stared at him. "Gilloon," I said, "Rogers and I and five other witnesses saw Hollowell inside the shed. . . ."

"Did you, Parker? The execution shed is lighted by lanterns. On a dark afternoon, during a thunderstorm, visibility is not reliable. And you were some forty feet from him. You saw an average-size man wearing a guard's uniform, with a guard's peaked cap drawn down over his forehead . . . a man you had no reason to assume was not Hollowell. You took his identity for granted."

"I can't dispute the logic of that," I said. "But if you're right that it wasn't Hollowell, who was it?"

"Teasdale, of course."

"Teasdale! For God's sake, man, if Teasdale assumed the identity of Hollowell, who did we see carried in as Teasdale?"

"No one," Gilloon said.

My mouth fell open. There was a moment of heavy silence. I

broke it finally by exclaiming: "Are you saying we did not see a man hanged at five o'clock this afternoon?"

"Precisely."

"Are you saying we were all victims of some sort of mass hallucination?"

"Certainly not. You saw what you believed to be Arthur Teasdale, just as you saw what you believed to be Hollowell. Again let me remind you . . . the lighting was poor and you had no reason at the time to suspect deception. But think back, Parker. What actually did you see? The shape of a man with a black hood covering his head, supported between two other men. But did you see that figure walk or hear it speak? Did you at any time discern an identifiable part of a human being, such as a hand or an exposed ankle?"

I squeezed my eyes shut for a moment, mentally re-examining the events in the shed. "No," I admitted. "I discerned nothing but the hood and the clothing and the shoes. But I did see him struggle at the foot of the gallows, and his body spasm on the trap. How do you explain that?"

"Simply. Like everything else, illusion. At a preconceived time Granger and Teasdale had only to slow their pace and jostle the figure with their own bodies to create the impression that the figure itself was resisting them. Teasdale alone used the same method on the trap."

"If it is your contention that the figure was some sort of dummy, I can't believe it, Gilloon. How could a dummy be made to vanish any more easily than a man?"

"It was not, strictly speaking, a dummy."

"Then what the devil was it?"

Gilloon held up a hand; he appeared to be enjoying himself immensely. "Do you recall my asking if Teasdale had a trade? You responded that he had worked in a textile mill, whereupon I asked if the prison textile mill stocked silk."

"Yes, yes, I recall that."

"Come now, Parker, use your imagination. What is one of the uses of silk . . . varnished silk?"

"I don't know," I began, but no sooner were the words past my lips than the answer sprang into my mind. "Good Lord . . . balloons!"

"Exactly."

"The figure we saw was a balloon?"

"In effect, yes. It is not difficult to sew and tie off a large piece of silk in the rough shape of a man. When inflated to a malleable state with helium or hydrogen, and seen in poor light from a distance of forty feet or better, while covered entirely by clothing and a hood, and weighted down with a pair of shoes and held tightly by two men . . . the effect can be maintained.

"The handiwork would have been done by Teasdale in the privacy of the death cell. The material was supplied from the prison textile mill by Granger. Once the sewing and tying had been accomplished, I imagine Granger took the piece out of the prison, varnished it, and returned it later. It need not have been inflated, naturally, until just prior to the execution. As to where the gas was obtained, I would think there would be a cylinder of hydrogen in the prison foundry."

I nodded.

"In any event, between four and five o'clock, when the three of them were alone in the death annex, Teasdale murdered Hollowell with an awl Granger had given him. Granger then transported Hollowell's body behind the stack of lumber a short distance away and probably also returned the gas cylinder to the foundry. The storm would have provided all the shield necessary, though even without it the risk was one worth taking.

"Once Granger and Teasdale had brought the balloon figure to the gallows, Granger, as hangman, placed the noose carefully around the head. You told me, Parker, that he was the last to examine the noose. While he was doing so, he inserted into the fibers that sharp sliver of wood you found in the trap cubicle. When he drew the noose taut, he made sure the sliver touched the balloon's surface so that when the trap was sprung and the balloon plunged downward the splinter would penetrate the silk. The sound of a balloon deflating is negligible. The storm made it more so. The dancing of the rope, of course, was caused by the escaping air.

"During the ensuing sixty seconds, the balloon completely deflated. There was nothing in the cubicle at that point except a bundle of clothing, silk, and shoes. The removal of all but the hood, to complete the trick, was a simple enough matter. You told me how it was done, when you mentioned the silvery glimmer you saw above the trap.

"That glimmer was a brief reflection of lantern light off a length of thin wire which had been attached to the clothing and to the balloon. Granger concealed the wire in his hand, and played out most of a seven or eight foot coil before he threw the trap lever.

"After he had gone to his knees with his back to the witness chairs, he merely opened the front of his duster and pulled up the bundle. No doubt it made something of a bulge, but the attention was focused on other matters. You did notice, Parker . . . and it was a helpful clue . . . that Granger appeared to be holding his stomach as if he were about to be ill. What he was actually doing was clutching the bundle so that it would not fall from beneath his duster. Later he hid the bundle among his belongings and transported it out of the prison when he went off duty. It was that bundle we saw burning in the fireplace in his cottage."

"But how did Teasdale get out of the prison?"

"The most obvious way imaginable," Gilloon said. "He walked out through the front gates."

"What!"

"Yes. Remember, he was wearing a guard's uniform . . . supplied by Granger . . . and there was a storm raging. I noticed when we first arrived tonight that the gateman seemed eager to return to his gatehouse, where it was dry. He scarcely looked at you and did not question me. That being the case, it's obvious that he would not have questioned someone who wore the proper uniform and kept his face averted as he gave Hollowell's name. The guards had not yet been alerted and the gateman would have no reason to suspect trickery.

"Once out, I suspect Teasdale simply took Granger's car and drove to Hainesville. When Granger himself came off duty, I would guess that he obtained a ride home with another guard, using some pretext to explain the absence of his own vehicle.

"I did not actually know, of course, that we would find Teasdale at Granger's place. I made a logical supposition in light of the other facts. Since Granger was the only other man alive who knew how the escape had been worked, I reasoned that an individual of Teasdale's stripe would not care to leave him alive and vulnerable to a confession, no matter what promises he might have made to Granger."

"If Teasdale managed his actual escape that easily, why did he choose to go through all that trickery with the balloon? Why didn't he just murder Hollowell, with Granger's help, and then leave the prison prior to the execution, between four and five?"

"Oh, I suppose he thought that the bizarre circumstances surrounding the disappearance of an apparently hanged man would insure him enough time to get clear of this immediate area. If you were confused and baffled, you would not sound an instant alarm, whereas you certainly would have if he had simply disappeared from his cell. Also, the prospect of leaving all of you a legacy of mystery and horror afforded him a warped sense of revenge."

"You're a brilliant man," I told him as I sank back in my chair.

Gilloon shrugged. "This kind of puzzle takes logic rather than brilliance, Parker. As I told you earlier tonight, it isn't always wise to discount the supernatural . . . but in a case where no clear evidence of the supernatural exits, the answer generally lies in some form of illusion. I've encountered a number of seemingly incredible occurrences, some of which were even more baffling than this one and most of which involved illusion. I expect I'll encounter others in the future as well."

"Why do you say that?"

"One almost seems able after a while to divine places where they will occur," he said matter-of-factly, "and therefore to make oneself available to challenge them."

I blinked at him. "Do you mean you intuited something like this would happen at Arrowmont Prison? That you have some sort of prevision?"

"Perhaps. Perhaps not. Perhaps I'm nothing more than a pulp writer who enjoys traveling." He gave me an enigmatic smile and got to his feet, clutching his notebooks. "I can't speak for you, Parker," he said, "but I seem to have acquired an intense thirst. You wouldn't happen to know where we might obtain a Guinness at this hour, would you?"

One week later, suddenly and without notice, Gilloon left Arrowmont Village. One day he was there, the next he was not. Where he went I do not know. I neither saw him nor heard of or from him again.

Who and what was Buckmaster Gilloon? Is it possible for one enigma to be attracted and motivated by another enigma? Can that which seems natural and coincidental be the result instead of preternatural forces? Perhaps you can understand now why these questions have plagued me in the sixty years since I knew him. And why I am haunted by that single passage I read by accident in his notebook, the passage that may hold the key to Buckmaster Gilloon:

If a jimbuck stands alone by the sea, on a night when the dark moon sings, how many grains of sand in a single one of his foot prints? . . .

Sweet Fever

Quarter before midnight, like on every evening except the Sabbath or when it's storming or when my rheumatism gets to paining too bad, me and Billy Bob went down to the Chigger Mountain railroad tunnel to wait for the night freight from St. Louis. This here was a fine summer evening, with a big old fat yellow moon hung above the pines on Hankers Ridge and mockingbirds and cicadas and toads making a soft ruckus. Nights like this, I have me a good feeling, hopeful, and I know Billy Bob does, too.

They's a bog hollow on the near side of the tunnel opening, and beside it a woody slope, not too steep. Halfway down the slope is a big catalpa tree, and that was where we always set, side-by-side with our backs up against the trunk.

So we come on down to there, me hobbling some with my cane and Billy Bob holding onto my arm. That moon was so bright you could see the melons lying in Ferdie Johnson's patch over on the left, and the rail tracks had a sleek oiled look coming out of the tunnel mouth and leading off toward the Sabreville yards a mile up the line. On the far side of the tracks, the woods and the run-down shacks that used to be a hobo jungle before the county sheriff closed it off thirty years back had them a silvery cast, like they was all coated in winter frost.

We set down under the catalpa tree and I leaned my head back to catch my wind. Billy Bob said: "Granpa, you feeling right?"

"Fine, boy."

"Rheumatism ain't started paining you?"

"Not a bit."

He give me a grin. "Got a little surprise for you."

"The hell you do."

"Fresh plug of blackstrap," he said. He come out of his pocket with it. "Mister Cotter got him in a shipment just today down at his store."

I was some pleased. But I said: "Now you hadn't ought to go spending your money on me, Billy Bob."

"Got nobody else I'd rather spend it on."

I took the plug and unwrapped it and had me a chew. Old man like me ain't got many pleasures left, but fresh blackstrap's one—good corn's another. Billy Bob gets us all the corn we need from Ben Logan's boys. They got a pretty good-size still up on Hankers Ridge, and their corn is the best in this part of the hills. Not that either of us is a drinking man, now. A little touch after supper and on special days is all. I never did hold with drinking too much, or doing anything too much, and I taught Billy Bob the same.

He's a good boy. Man couldn't ask for a better grandson. But I raised him that way—in my own image, you might say—after both my own son Rufus and Billy Bob's ma got taken from us in 1947. I reckon I done a right job of it, and I couldn't be less proud of him than I was of his pa, or love him no less, either.

Well, we set there and I worked on the chew of blackstrap and had a spit every now and then, and neither of us said much. Pretty soon the first whistle come, away off on the other side of Chigger Mountain. Billy Bob cocked his head and said: "She's right on schedule."

"Mostly is," I said, "this time of year."

That sad lonesome hungry ache started up in me again— what my daddy used to call the "sweet fever". He was a railroad man, and I grew up around trains and spent a goodly part of my early years at the roundhouse in the Sabreville yards. Once, when I was ten, he let me take the throttle of the big 2-8-0 Mogul steam locomotive on his highballing run to Eulalia, and I can't recollect no more finer experience in my whole life. Later on I worked as a callboy, and then as a fireman on a 2-10-4, and put in some time as a yard tender engineer, and I expect I'd have gone on in railroading if it hadn't been for the Depression and getting myself married and having Rufus. My daddy's short-line company folded up in 1931, and half a dozen others, too, and wasn't no work for either of us in Sabreville or Eulalia or anywheres else on the iron. That squeezed the will right out of him, and he took to ailing, and I had to accept a job on Mr. John Barnett's truck farm to support him and the rest of my family. Was my intention to go back into railroading, but the Depression dragged on, and my daddy died, and a year later my wife Amanda took sick and passed on, and by the time the war come it was just too late.

But Rufus got him the sweet fever, too, and took a switch-man's job in the Sabreville yards, and worked there right up until the night he died. Billy Bob was only three then; his own sweet fever comes most purely from me and what I taught him. Ain't no doubt trains been a major part of all our lives, good and bad, and ain't no doubt, neither, they get into a man's blood and maybe change him, too, in one way and another. I reckon they do.

The whistle come again, closer now, and I judged the St. Louis freight was just about to enter the tunnel on the other side of the mountain. You could hear the big wheels singing on the track, and, if you listened close, you could just about hear the banging of couplings and the hiss of air brakes as the engineer throttled down for the curve. The tunnel don't run straight through Chigger Mountain; she comes in from the north and angles to the east, so that a big freight like the St. Louis got to cut back to quarter speed coming through.

When she entered the tunnel, the tracks down below seemed to shimmy, and you could feel the vibration clear up where we was sitting under the catalpa tree. Billy Bob stood himself up and peered down toward the black tunnel mouth like a bird dog on a point. The whistle come again, and once more, from inside the tunnel, sounding hollow and miseried now. Every time I heard it like that, I thought of a body trapped and hurting and crying out for help that wouldn't come in the empty hours of the night. I swallowed and shifted the cud of blackstrap and worked up a spit to keep my mouth from drying. The sweet fever feeling was strong in my stomach.

The blackness around the tunnel opening commenced to lighten, and got brighter and brighter until the long white glow from the locomotive's headlamp spilled out onto the tracks beyond. Then she come through into my sight, her light shining like a giant's eye, and the engineer give another tug on the whistle, and the sound of her was a clattering rumble as loud to my ears as a mountain rock slide. But she wasn't moving fast, just kind of easing along, pulling herself out of that tunnel like a nightcrawler out of a mound of earth.

The locomotive *clacked* on past, and me and Billy Bob watched her string slide along in front of us. Flats, boxcars, three tankers in a row, more flats loaded down with pine logs big around as a privy, a refrigerator car, five coal gondolas, another link of boxcars. *Fifty in the string already,* I thought. *She won't be dragging more than sixty, sixty-five. . . .*

Billy Bob said suddenly: "Granpa, look yonder!"

He had his arm up, pointing. My eyes ain't so good no more, and it took me a couple of seconds to follow his point, over on our left and down at the door of the third boxcar in the last link. It was sliding open, and clear in the moonlight I saw a man's head come out, then his shoulders.

"It's a floater, Granpa," Billy Bob said, excited. "He's gonna jump. Look at him holding there . . . he's gonna jump."

I spit into the grass. "Help me up, boy."

He got a hand under my arm and lifted me up and held me until I was steady on my cane. Down there at the door of the boxcar, the floater was looking both ways along the string of cars and down at the ground beside the tracks. That ground was soft loam, and the train was going slow enough that there wasn't much chance he would hurt himself jumping off. He come to that same idea, and, as soon as he did, he flung himself off the car with his arms spread out and his hair and coattails flying in the slipstream. I saw him land solid and go down and roll over once. Then he knelt there, shaking his head a little, looking around.

Well, he was the first floater we'd seen in seven months. The yard crews seal up the cars nowadays, and they ain't many ride the rails anyhow, even down in our part of the country. But every now and then a floater wants to ride bad enough to break a seal, or hides himself in a gondola or on a loaded flat. Kids, old-time hoboes, wanted men. They's still a few.

And some of 'em get off right down where this one had, because they know the St. Louis freight stops in Sabreville and they's yardmen there that check the string, or because they see the run-down shacks of the old hobo jungle or Ferdie Johnson's melon patch. Man rides a freight long enough, no provisions, he gets mighty hungry; the sight of a melon patch like Ferdie's is plenty enough to make him jump off.

"Billy Bob," I said.

"Yes, Granpa. You wait easy now."

He went off along the slope, running. I watched the floater, and he come up on his feet and got himself into a clump of bushes alongside the tracks to wait for the caboose to pass so's he wouldn't be seen. Pretty soon the last of the cars left the tunnel, and then the caboose with a signalman holding a red-eye lantern out on the platform. When she was down the tracks and just about beyond my sight, the floater showed himself again and had him another look around. Then, sure enough, he made straight for the melon patch.

Once he got into it, I couldn't see him, because he was in close to the woods at the edge of the slope. I couldn't see Billy Bob, neither. The whistle sounded one final time, mournful, as the lights of the caboose disappeared, and a chill come to my neck and set there like a cold dead hand. I closed my eyes and listened to the last singing of the wheels fade away.

It weren't long before I heard footfalls on the slope coming near, then the angry sound of a stranger's voice, but I kept my eyes shut until they walked up close and Billy Bob said: "Granpa." When I opened 'em, the floater was standing three feet in front of me, white face shining in the moonlight—scared face, angry face, evil face.

"What the hell is this?" he said. "What you want with me?"

"Give me your gun, Billy Bob," I said.

He did it, and I held her tight and lifted the barrel. The ache in my stomach was so strong my knees felt weak and I could scarcely breathe. But my hand was steady.

The floater's eyes come wide open and he backed off a step. "Hey," he said, "hey, you can't. . . ."

I shot him twice.

He fell over and rolled some and come up on his back. They wasn't no doubt he was dead, so I give the gun back to Billy Bob and he put it away in his belt. "All right, boy," I said.

Billy Bob nodded and went over and hoisted the dead floater onto his shoulder. I watched him trudge off toward the bog hollow, and in my mind I could hear the train whistle as she'd sounded from inside the tunnel. I thought again, as I had so many times, that it was the way my boy Rufus and Billy Bob's ma must have sounded that night in 1947, when the two float-ers from the hobo jungle broke into their home and raped her and shot Rufus to death. She lived just long enough to tell us about the floaters, but they was never caught. So it was up to me, and then up to me and Billy Bob when he come of age.

Well, it ain't like it once was, and that saddens me. But they's still a few that ride the rails, still a few take it into their heads to jump off down there when the St. Louis freight slows coming through the Chigger Mountain tunnel.

Oh my, yes, they'll always be a few for me and Billy Bob and the sweet fever inside us both.

Righteous Guns

It was hot.

And quiet—too quiet.

He walked slowly along the dusty street, one hand resting on the Colt Peacemaker pouched at his hip. The harsh midday sun made the false-fronted buildings stand out in sharp relief against a sky more white than blue, like an alkali flat turned upside down. Heat mirage shimmered beyond the livery stable in the next block, half obscuring the road that led up into the foothills west of town.

He paused opposite the Lucky Lady Saloon and Gambling Hall and stood hip-shot, listening to the silence. Nothing moved anywhere ahead of him or around him. There were no horses tied to the hitch rails, no wagons or buckboards, no townspeople making their way along the plank sidewalks. But he could feel eyes watching him from behind closed doors and shuttered windows.

Waiting, all of them—just as he was.

Waiting for the lawmen and their righteous guns.

Sweat worked its way out from under his Stetson; he wiped it away with the back of his left hand, smearing the dust cake on his lean, sun-weathered face. His mouth tasted dry and dusty, like the street itself, and he thought of pushing in through the saloon's batwings for a beer and a shot of rye. But liquor dulled a man's thoughts, turned his reflexes slow. No liquor today.

From his shirt pocket he took out the makings and rolled a

cigarette with his left hand. He scratched a sulphur match into flame on the sole of his boot. His right hand didn't move from the butt of his Peacemaker in its hand-tooled Mexican holster.

How many of them would there be? Close to a dozen, likely, maybe more. Robbing the Cattlemen's and Merchant's Bank as he'd done this morning, shooting down the bank director, Leo Furman, in cold blood when he wouldn't open the safe—those were about as serious crimes as there were in the territory. There'd be plenty in the posse, all right. They'd want him bad, them and their righteous guns.

Not that it mattered much, he thought. A wry smile bent the corners of his mouth. He'd faced lawmen before, in numbers from one to twenty, in towns like this one in half a dozen states and territories throughout the West. This was nothing new. This was just more of the same for a man like him.

It was only a question of time. He'd wait, because there was nothing else for him to do. He hadn't got the money from the bank; Leo Furman had tried for a hide-out gun and he'd had to shoot him before Furman could open the safe. So the only thing he could do was wait. Better to face them here, than run and have them chase him down like a dog.

When they came, he'd be ready for them.

He blew smoke into the hot still air, and then commenced walking again, thinking about Leo Furman. A bossy, fussy man, like so many bank directors, he'd thought that the money other men entrusted to him gave him power over those men. Demanding, high and mighty, full of contempt—that was Furman. He wasn't sorry he'd killed the bastard. He wasn't sorry at all.

He moved on past Benson's Mercantile, the Elite Café, the Palace Hotel. There was still no sound, nothing stirring in the thick, milky heat. It was as if the town itself was holding its breath now.

On past the Eternal Rest Funeral Home, the blacksmith's

shop, the deserted sheriff's office, heading toward the hostler's. He knew just what a menacing figure he cut, moving along that dusty, barren street—big, hard face full of angles and shadows, body leaned down to sinew and bone. Most men stood aside when he passed, avoiding his eyes. So did the women. They were afraid of him, the women; the only way he'd ever had one was by money or by force.

Sometimes, late at night, he would wake up in a strange bed or by the remains of a trailside fire and think of what might have been. An end to the vicious swath he cut through the West; an end to the shooting and the killing of decent men; righteous guns instead of his own desperate ones, or, better yet, no guns at all. The love of a good woman, a small ranch on good grazing land. . . .

Something moved in the alley between the blacksmith's shop and the livery.

A shadow, then a second shadow.

He tensed, alert to the sudden smell of danger. He slowed to a walk, pitched his cigarette away, let his fingers curl loosely around the butt of his Peacemaker. Squinted through the hard glare of the sunlight.

More movement inside the alley. Over on the far side of the street, too, behind Baldwin's Feed and Grain Store. Furtive sounds reached his ears: the soft sliding of boots in the dust, the faint *thump* of an arm or hand or leg against wood.

They were here.

Most times they came openly, riding in on their horses, weapons at the ready. Once in a while, though, they came in quiet and slinking like this, to wait in ambush in the shadows. No better than he was, then. In their own way, just as desperate.

Well, it didn't matter.

It was time, and, as always, he was ready.

"Hold it right there, Gaines!" a voice roared suddenly from the alley. "We've got you surrounded!"

He bent his knees and let himself bow slightly at the middle. But he was scowling now. Gaines, the voice had said. How did they know his real name?

"You can't get away, Gaines! Stand where you are and raise your hands over your head!"

There was something about that voice, the odd thunderous tone of it, as if it were coming through a megaphone, that made him feel suddenly uneasy. More than uneasy—strange, dizzy. His head began to ache. The sun-baked street, the false-fronted buildings, seemed to shift in and out of focus, to take on new and different dimensions. *Sunstroke,* he thought. *I been standing out here in the heat too long.*

But it wasn't sunstroke. . . .

One of the shadows in the alley shifted into view—his first clear glimpse of the law. And he stared, for the law dog wasn't wearing Levi's or broad-brimmed hat or tin star pinned to vest or cotton shirt, wasn't carrying Winchester rifle or Colt six-gun. Strange blue uniform, blue helmet, weapon in one hand like none he'd ever seen before.

He stood blinking, confused. And saw then that the buildings didn't just have false fronts; they had false backs, too, and no backs at all on some of them, just a latticework of wooden supports like sets in a play.

Sets in a movie.

Movie sets, TV-show sets on the back lot of Mammoth Pictures.

A dozen movies, a hundred TV shows, all starring Roy Gaines in the rôle of the villain—and Leo Furman, the director, always telling him what to do, treating him with contempt, never once letting him be good and decent, never once letting him be the hero—wouldn't open his safe, wouldn't give him the money he needed to pay his gambling debts, and so he'd shot Furman dead, just as he would any damned fool who crossed him—and then he'd come here, because there was no place else for him to go, a man on the run, killer on the run, here to make still another last stand. . . .

"Gaines! You can't escape! Raise your hands over your head! Don't make us do this the hard way!"

The hard way, the hard way, the hard way. . . .

There was a jolting in his mind; the false-fronted buildings, the sun-blasted street settled back into familiar focus. Then, ahead, he could see four, five, six of the posse men fanning out toward him, keeping to cover. A grim smile formed on his mouth. He'd done all this before, so many times before. He knew just what to do. He didn't even have to think about it.

"All right," he yelled, "come and get it, boys!" His hand went down, came up again with his desperate gun blazing. . . .

And the righteous guns cut him down.

FLOOD

She sat at the upstairs bedroom window, watching the river run wildly below. Rain lay like crinkled cellophane wrap on the glass, so that everything outside seemed shimmery, distorted—the low-hanging, black-veined clouds, the half-submerged trees along the banks, the drift and wreckage riding the churning brown flood waters. She could hear the sound of the water, a constantly thrumming pulse, even with the rain beating a furious tattoo on the roof.

Nearly a week now of steady downpour, a chain of Pacific storms that had lashed northern California with winds up to 100 miles per hour. It seemed to her that it had been raining much longer, that she could not remember a time when the sky was clear and blue and the sun shone. The rain was inside her, too. When she looked into the mirror, looked into her own eyes, what she saw was a wet, gray, swampy place, a sodden landscape like the one she watched through the window. One in which she was trapped, as she was physically trapped here and now. One from which there seemed to be no escape.

She shivered; it was cold in the room. They had been without heat or power for more than twenty-four hours. The fierce storm winds had toppled trees and power lines everywhere in the region. Roads were inundated and blocked by mudslides, one of them River Road fifty yards west of their house. Flood stage along these low-lying areas was thirty-two feet; the rising water had reached that mark at 8:00 last night, hours after the evacuation orders had been issued. It must be above forty feet now, at 2:00 in the afternoon. All the rooms downstairs were flooded halfway to their ceilings. The last time she'd looked, the car was totally covered and the only parts of the deck still visible were the tops of the support poles for the latticework roof. The roof itself had long since been torn off and carried away.

From the pocket of her pea jacket, as she had several times during the day, she took the ivory scrimshaw bowl. Smooth, round, heavy-bottomed, it fitted exactly the palm of her hand. Her grandfather had carved it from a walrus tusk and done the lacy scrimshawing in his spare time, during the period he'd worked as a mail carrier in Nome just after the Alaska gold rush. He'd given it to her mother, who in turn had passed it on to her only daughter. It had been the first thing she'd grabbed to bring upstairs with her when the inpouring water forced them to abandon the lower floor. It was all she owned of any value, as Darrell so often reminded her.

"You and that damn' bowl," he'd said this morning. "Well, you might as well hang onto it. We may need whatever we can sell it for someday. Nothing else of yours is worth half as much, God knows."

She stroked the cold surface, the intricate black pattern. It gave her comfort. Her only comfort in times of unhappiness and stress.

Shadows crawled thickly in the room—moist shadows laden with the brown-slime smell of the river. She found it difficult to breathe, but opening the window to let in fresh air would only worsen the stench. She thought of relighting one of the candles, to keep the shadows at bay, but the unsteady flame reflected off the windowpane and made it even harder for her to see out. She was not sure why she wanted to keep looking out, but she did, and she had all through the day. Compelled to sit here and watch the rain beat down, the murky, churning water rise higher and higher.

There would be another rescue boat along soon, maybe even one of the evacuation helicopters that were brought in when the flood waters grew too dangerous for small craft. Rio Lomas, three miles to the east, had been cut off even longer than the River Road homes had, almost a day and a half; by now, they would be airlifting evacuees to one of the larger towns inland, at a safe distance from the river. She wished that was where she was, in one of those towns, in an emergency shelter where she could be warm and dry, where the lights were bright and there was clean air to breathe.

Empty wish. Darrell wouldn't leave when the rescuers showed up. No matter how bad things were then, he wouldn't budge. He had refused evacuation in 1986, the worst flood in the river's history, when the waters crested at better than forty-eight feet. They had both come close to drowning that year, forced at the last to sit huddled in the attic crawl space with the last dozen of his paintings wrapped in plastic sheeting like corpses awaiting burial. He'd refused to leave five years ago as well, the last time before this that the river had overrun its banks and made an island of their home. Stubborn. Fiercely possessive. Yes, and so many other less than endearing traits. So many others.

She rubbed the scrimshaw bowl and watched the rain slant down, the turmoil of conflicting currents and weird boils and eddy lines in the main channel, the soapy yellowish-white foam that scudded along what was left of the banks.

Why am I here? she thought. *I don't want to be here. I haven't wanted to be here in a long, long time.*

The old, tired lament. And the old, tired response to it: *I have nowhere else to go. Mom and Pop both gone, Jack blown up by a land mine in Vietnam, no other siblings or aunts or uncles or even a cousin. A few casual friends but none I can turn to, talk to, count on.*

Twenty-one years with Darrell, exactly half my life, and the twenty-one before him so far removed I can scarcely remember them. Where would I go? What could I do?

Sudden crashing noise from the far end of the house—Darrell's studio. He'd been drinking all day, and now he had reached the mean tantrum stage where he began breaking things. Splintering, tearing sounds reached her ears; he was at his paintings again. Not the better, finished ones. He never destroyed those oils and watercolors, no matter how drunk or frustrated or enraged he became, because they were his "true art"—the ones he believed were the work of an undiscovered, unappreciated genius, the ones he bitterly hoped to sell to summer tourists and the handful of local collectors, so they could pay their bills or at least keep their credit from being cut off altogether. No, his destructive wrath was reserved for the unfinished canvases, his false starts, and for the unsold riverscapes and still-lifes and portraits of eccentric river dwellers that he'd decided were expendable, not quite up to his own lofty standards.

At first she, too, had believed he was a genius. A great and sensitive visionary. In those early days she had wanted to be an artist herself, at least an artisan. Not painting, nothing so important as that, just the designer and maker of earrings and pendants and other jewelry. She'd felt sure she had the talent to excel at this, but he had convinced her otherwise. Ridiculed and disparaged her efforts until, finally, she'd lost all enthusiasm and given up her work, her dreams, everything except her day-to-day existence as Mrs. Darrell Boyd. But he'd succeeded not only in disillusioning her about her own abilities, but in giving her a true perspective on his as well. He was far less gifted than he considered himself to be, at best a shade or two above mediocre.

The description fit their marriage just as aptly. At best it had been a shade or two above mediocre. At worst. . . .

Footsteps in the hallway, hard and lurching. She sat rigid, staring out through the rain-wavy glass. Waiting, steeling herself.

"Hey! Hey, you in there!"

She no longer had a name in her own house. She had become Hey or Hey, You or harsh epithets just as impersonal.

"You hear me? I'm talking to you."

"I hear you, Darrell." Slowly she turned her head. He stood slouched in the doorway, shirt mostly unbuttoned and pulled free of his Levi's so that the bulge of his paunch showed. Unshaven, red-eyed, his graying hair a finger-rubbed tangle. She noticed all of that, and yet it was as though she were seeing him the way she had been seeing the storm-savaged river, through a pane of wavy glass. She looked away again before she said: "What do you want?"

"What d'you think I want?"

"I'm not a mind-reader."

"What'd you do with it? Where'd you hide it this time?"

"Hide what?"

"You know what. Don't give me that."

"I don't touch your liquor. I never have."

"The hell you never have. There's another fifth. I brought it upstairs myself. What'd you do with it?"

"Look in the storeroom. That's where you put it."

"I know where I put it. Where'd *you* put it?"

"I never touched it, Darrell."

"Liar! Bitch!"

She didn't respond. Outside, something swirled past on the cocoa-brown water—a dead animal of some kind, a goat or large dog. She couldn't be sure because it was there one instant, bobbing and partly submerged, and the next it was gone.

"Where's that bottle, god damn it? I'm warning you."

"In the storeroom," she said.

"That where you hid it?"

"It's been there all along."

"You go find it. Right now, you hear me?"

"I hear you."

"Now. Right this minute."

She got to her feet, not hurrying. Without looking at him she started across the room.

"And put that silly damn' bowl away," he said. "Why d'you always have to keep playing with that thing, petting it like it's a fetish or something?"

She slipped the scrimshawed ivory back into her pocket, walked past him into the hallway. Each step was an effort, somehow, as if her legs—like the land, like the house itself—had become water-logged.

The storeroom was between the bedroom and his studio. It had started out as her work space, but when she'd given up jewelry-making, it had gradually evolved into a catch-all storage area. Boxes, oddments of furniture, unused canvases crowded it now, along with dust and spider webs. When they'd abandoned the lower floor this morning, she had brought up as much food as they might need and whatever else could be salvaged, and put it in there. The perishables were on melting ice in the big cooler, the rest scattered on boxes and on the floor. She poked listlessly among the food items and cartons, while he watched from the doorway. It took her less than a minute to find his last fifth of Scotch, more or less in plain sight behind the leg of a discarded table. She picked it up, held it out to him.

He snatched it from her hand. "Don't you ever do that again. Understand? You hide liquor from me again, you'll be sorry."

"All right," she said.

"Make me a sandwich," he said. "I'm hungry."

"What kind of sandwich?"

"What do I care what kind? A sandwich."

"All right."

"Make yourself useful for a change," he said, and stalked off with the bottle cradled like an infant against his chest.

She buttered bread, layered ham and processed cheese on top, and then spread mustard on a second slice. Did it all mechanically, taking her time. She put the sandwich on a paper plate and brought it to the studio.

He was over by the tall double windows, squinting at one of his older riverscapes—trying to decide whether or not to destroy it, probably. He seemed even more misshapen and indistinct to her now, as if there was more than glass between them, as if she were looking at him underwater. She set the sandwich on his worktable, between the jars of oil paint and the now open fifth of Scotch, and retreated to the hallway.

The open door to the bathroom drew her. She went inside and close to the medicine cabinet mirror, but it was too dark to make out her image clearly. She lit a candle and held it up. Her face, like his, seemed water-distorted, and, when she peered at it from an inch or so away, she could see the rain in her eyes. Behind her eyes. Rain and a turbulent, rising cataract like the one outside.

She snuffed the candle, returned to the bedroom, and her seat before the window. Rising, yes. The river's surface was a ferment spotted with débris—clumps of uprooted brush, logs, and tree limbs bobbing drunkenly, a fence rail, the shattered remains of a rowboat, a child's red wagon. One of the logs slammed against the side wall of the house with enough force to crack boards, before it swirled away.

The rain continued to beat down in gray metallic sheets. The dark waters roared and shrieked like a wild creature caught in a snare, ripping at what was left of its banks, tearing them down and apart in a frenzy. She could feel the flood, cold, slimy on her face and the backs of her hands. Smell and taste it, too, rank and primitive.

And still the waters kept rising. . . .

Abruptly she stood. On heavy legs, her mind blank, she went out and back to Darrell's studio. He was sitting hunched at the worktable, staring fixedly into a tumbler of whiskey, the sandwich she'd made uneaten and pushed aside. His portable radio was on, tuned to a Santa Rosa station, the voice of a newscaster droning words that had no meaning for her. He did not hear her as she stepped up behind him; he had no idea she was there.

You've never known I was here, she thought. Just that one thought. Then her mind was blank again.

She took out the scrimshaw bowl, held it bottom side up in her hand. She no longer heard the newscast; she listened instead to the roaring and shrieking of the flood. Then, without hesitation, she raised the bowl and brought it down with all her strength on the back of his head.

He didn't make a sound. Or, if he did, the raging of the waters drowned it out.

She had no difficulty dragging him across to the window. It was as if, dead or dying, he had become almost weightless. The wind flailed her with rain and surface spume as she raised the sash, hoisted him onto the sill. The river was only a few feet below, all but filling the downstairs rooms; it boiled and frothed, creating little whirlpools clogged with flotsam. She pushed Darrell down into the brown turmoil. There was a splash, and two or three seconds later, no more than that, he wasn't there any more.

She was seated once again at the bedroom window when the rescue boat appeared. By then, mercifully, it had stopped raining and the flood waters did not seem to be rising any longer. The worst was over. Everything was still gray and moist and chaotic, but there was a hint of clearing light in the grayness. She was sure of it—light outside and inside, both.

When she saw the boat rounding the bend, she opened the window and waved her arms to show the rescuers where she was. They came straight to her at accelerated speed, two men wearing neoprene wetsuits hunched in the stern. She knew both of them; they were volunteer firemen in Rio Lomas.

As they drew alongside, one of them called out: "Are you all right, Missus Boyd?"

She touched the freshly polished ivory bowl in her pocket. It was not the only thing of value she had; it never had been. "My name is Lee Anne," she said. "Lee Anne Meeker. Jewelry maker."

"Are you all right?"

"Yes, I'm all right"

"Where's your husband?"

"Gone," she said.

"Gone? What do you mean . . . gone?"

She was not a liar; she told them the literal and absolute truth. "The flood took him," she said. "He was swept away in the flood."

CHRISTMAS GIFTS

Matt Hollis was still a few miles from his uncle's ranch when the snowstorm started. The winter sky had been clear when he'd set out from Auburn in mid-afternoon. But the clouds had piled up rapidly, getting thicker and darker-veined until the whole sky was the color of coal smoke. The wind had sharpened to an icy breath that buffeted the rented wagon and roan horse. Now, as an early dusk approached, the snow flurries had come abruptly—big flakes swirled by the wind so that the pine forest flanking the trail was a misty blur.

The hostler in Auburn had warned him that this might happen; it often did in late December in the High Sierra foothills. He'd been offered a bed for the night in the stable, but the prospect hadn't appealed to Matt. He'd already spent too many uncomfortable nights on the long westward train trip from Kansas.

Uncle Jake and Aunt Ella weren't expecting him until tomorrow, Christmas Eve, which was why he hadn't been met at Auburn's tiny depot. It was just as well, Matt had thought. He was no longer a boy who needed to be met and escorted. He was fifteen, strong from farm work and plenty capable of traveling alone and finding his own way.

Whether he arrived early or not, the Boyds wouldn't be pleased to see him. Uncle Jake's letters had made it plain he was taking Matt in only because this was the final wish of his sister, Matt's mother. By the same token Matt had come West only because Ma had made him promise to spend at least one Christmas with his aunt and uncle. She'd put a lot of stock in family, and it was the least he could do to honor her memory.

He sat huddled inside his fleece-lined long coat, mittens, and cap, feeling sad and very much alone. His thoughts kept returning to the Kansas plains, to the farm where he'd been born in 1875 and that had been sold for taxes last month. To Christmases past, when both his folks were alive and they'd had bountiful crops of wheat and corn. Every holiday dinner had been a feast then. Baked turkey and skillet-browned cush—a mixture of wheat bread and cornmeal soaked in hot water, then fried with raisins and spices. Sweet potatoes glazed with sorghum. Biscuits smothered in wild plum jelly. Ma's special dried peach cobbler. . . .

The prospect of Christmas in this unfamiliar mountain wilderness, with Pa and Ma and the farm all gone, was a cheerless one. He'd never met Aunt Ella or Uncle Jake; he was a baby when they had moved to California. Ma had said they were good people, honest and hard-working, and that they'd be glad for his company, but Uncle Jake's cold letters made Matt believe otherwise. He would stay with them no later than spring, he'd decided. Then he'd go back to Kansas.

Time passed in a white swirl. Just how much Matt wasn't sure. Finally the road crested and began to descend along the rim of a snow-skinned meadow. The wind was even fiercer here, without one wall of trees to deflect its force. Ice particles clung to his eyebrows, kept trying to freeze his eyelids shut. It couldn't be much farther to the ranch, could it?

Darkness was settling around him when he saw the faint shimmer of light ahead. He scrubbed at his eyes, leaning forward. The glow was off to his left, close to the trail, else he wouldn't have been able to see it at all.

A little farther on, tall fence posts marked the ranch lane. He gigged the weary roan between the posts and through soft, shallow drifts. Sturdy buildings took on shape as he approached: log house, barn, corral, and an open-sided lean-to, a shed-like outbuilding barely visible beyond the barn. The lamplight came from behind the house's frost-rimmed windows.

Matt halted at the front gate, took his carpetbag from the wagon bed, and slogged to the door. He could've shouted himself hoarse before anyone inside heard him. So he tried the latch, found the door unbarred, and let the wind push him inside.

The big front room was deserted. He leaned back against the door to shut it, then called out: "Uncle Jake, Aunt Ella! It's Matt Hollis!"

No one answered.

Matt stood scraping snow cake off his face, slapping it from his clothing. The room was warm from a now-banked fire on the hearth. Two lamps were lit here, another in the kitchen beyond. Mistletoe and holly berries hung festively from the rafters, and near the hearth was a cut spruce decorated with red paper and red candles, snippets of cotton, and a five-pointed star. He was surprised to see three white stockings tacked to the mantelpiece. His aunt and uncle had no children.

A rich, spicy smell drew him into the kitchen. It, too, was empty. The puncheon table was set for two, and on the cast-iron stove a pot of stew was cooking. Almost all the gravy had boiled away, Matt saw, and the rest was close to burning. Frowning, he moved the pot to a far edge.

"Aunt Ella! Uncle Jake!"

Only the wind answered him, howling along the eaves.

Quickly Matt searched the other three rooms. One of them—not the smallest—evidently would be his; it contained a comfortable-looking trundle bed made up with a thick quilt.

There was no sign of the Boyds there or anywhere else in the house.

A sense of wrongness sent him hurrying out again into the ice-bound darkness. He led the shivering roan to the barn, and, as he neared the building, he saw that one of the door halves had been blown open and was banging in the wind. Inside it was pitch black.

He unlatched the other half, prodded horse and wagon inside, then forced both halves shut. A sulphur match from his emergency supply showed him a windproof railroad lantern on a wall hook. He lighted the wick, stood looking around at more emptiness.

Where were the Boyds? What had happened here tonight?

Matt hurriedly unharnessed the roan, led it to one of the stalls. Then, carrying the lantern, he bent his lean body once more into the wild white smother outside. Flinty snow half blinded him as he slogged to the corral. The wind all but took his breath away.

When he reached the lean-to, he found a plow horse and a saddle horse huddled together at the rear. They should have been in the barn, not here where they would eventually freeze.

Really worried now, Matt fought his way back toward the barn. The snowfall had already covered his tracks, and this turned out to be a blessing. If he hadn't taken a slightly differ-ent route, he might never have seen the snow-mantled shape pressed against the barn's side wall.

At first he thought it was a barrel or maybe a plow, but still he detoured that way for a closer look. He was almost upon it, before the lantern light showed him a slumped human form. The white-iced face inside a fur-lined parka hood was a woman's. Matt cried—"Aunt Ella!"—but the eyes remained frozen shut. He felt the artery in her neck, and relief flooded him when his fingers found a faint pulse.

He lifted and cradled her in his arms, a small woman who weighed hardly more than a hundredweight sack of flour. Even so he was staggering by the time he reached the house.

Inside he put her gently on the hearth, took off her wet clothing, and wrapped her in a buffalo robe from the Boyds' bedroom. He piled logs on the fire until it was blazing, boiled water in the kitchen, and brewed tea. It seemed to take a long time for her to regain her senses. At last her eyelids fluttered open. She stared up at him blankly.

"It's me, Aunt Ella. Matt. Here, drink this."

He fed her little sips of steaming tea until the blueness left her lips and she was able to speak. "Matt. Oh, thank the Lord. Your uncle . . . did you find him?"

"No. Where is he?"

"Smokehouse behind the barn. He has a head wound, and his leg may be broken."

In swift, halting sentences she told Matt what had happened. Uncle Jake had gone out just before the storm began, to put the horses in the barn. One spooked and broke loose, and he chased it into the apple orchard near the smokehouse, where he tripped and fell, twisting his leg and hitting his head. When he didn't come back, Aunt Ella went looking for him. By then he had crawled part way to the smokehouse, but he was dazed and in too much pain to walk. She helped him the rest of the way into the building, then started back to the house for blankets. But the storm had worsened by then and most of her strength was gone. The last thing she remembered was leaning against the barn to rest for a few seconds.

"I wasn't able to wedge the smokehouse door shut all the way," she told Matt. "Jake's liable to freeze in there, hurt the way he is, if we don't get him out soon!"

"I'll go for him, Aunt Ella. You stay here where it's warm."

She nodded, shivering. "There's a sleigh in the barn. We use it for fetching firewood logs."

Carrying two heavy wool blankets, Matt once again braved the storm's fury. He found the sleigh, and dragged it from the barn. Locating the smokehouse took longer. He could feel his own strength ebbing when it finally materialized ahead. Drifts were piled high against the partly open door, but the snow was still powdery enough for him to clear it away with his mittened hands. Uncle Jake lay curled on the floor inside, unconscious but still breathing.

Matt wasn't sure afterward how long it took him to lift the heavy body onto the sleigh, swaddle it in the blankets, and haul it outside. The long dragging trek back to the house was another timeless blur. Only fear for his uncle and him freezing to death kept Matt's tired legs moving through the now deep drifts.

At long last the house lights appeared mistily, and then he was at the door and Aunt Ella was helping him carry Uncle Jake inside. Sinking down before the warmth of the fire was the last thing he knew. . . .

In the morning, when he awoke in the trundle bed, the storm was over and the day before Christmas sparkled, silver and white under a pale sun. Every muscle in his body ached, but he felt well enough otherwise. He smelled coffee and frying bacon, and shortly Aunt Ella brought him his breakfast on a tray. Her face glistened with salve applied to patches of frostbite.

"Frostbite's not too bad," she told him. "You brought me inside just in time. Your Uncle Jake, too. His leg's fractured, but it's a clean break, and his head wound's not serious. He's eager to see you as soon as you're up and dressed."

Matt nodded. "I'm just glad I arrived a day early," he said, "and that I decided not to stay overnight in Auburn."

"So are we, son. Mighty glad and grateful." Aunt Ella sat beside him as he sipped hot coffee. "But don't you think saving our lives is the only reason. We've been looking forward to having you here ever since your poor ma first wrote us about it."

"You have? But I thought . . . I mean, Uncle Jake didn't seem too happy about it in his letters."

"*Pshaw.* Jake never was any good at putting his true feelings on paper, and I'm no better. Why, having you live with us will be a joy. We were never blessed with children, and . . . well, it'll be like having a son of our own. You're the best Christmas present we could've been given."

Matt remembered the festive decorations, the three stockings on the mantelpiece, the welcoming way his room had been made up, and he knew Aunt Ella was telling the truth. A part of him felt ashamed for his bitter thoughts about the Boyds. Another part felt warm and happy for the first time since Ma's passing.

He hadn't just given special holiday gifts; he'd received some, too. A new home and family, and a new appreciation of the season's spirit.

This would be a fine Christmas after all.

FERGUS O'HARA, DETECTIVE

On a balmy March afternoon in the third full year of the War Between the States, while that conflict continued to rage bloodily some 2,000 miles distant, Fergus and Hattie O'Hara jostled their way along San Francisco's Embarcadero toward Long Wharf and the riverboat, *Delta Star*. The half-plank, half-dirt roads and plank walks were choked with horses, mules, cargo-laden wagons—and with all manner of humanity: bearded miners and burly roustabouts and sun-darkened farmers; rope-muscled Kanakas and Filipino laborers and coolie-hatted Chinese; shrewd-eyed merchants and ruffle-shirted gamblers and bonneted ladies who might have been the wives of prominent citizens or trollops on their way to the gold fields of the Mother Lode. Both the pace and the din were furious. At exactly 4:00p.m. some twenty steamers would leave the waterfront, bound upriver for Sacramento and Stockton and points in between.

O'Hara clung to their carpetbags and Hattie clung to O'Hara as they pushed through the throng. They could see the *Delta Star* the moment they reached Long Wharf. She was an impressive side-wheeler, one of the "floating palaces" that had adorned the Sacramento and San Joaquin rivers for more than ten years. Powered by a single-cylinder, vertical-beam engine, she was 245 feet long and had slim, graceful lines. The long rows of windows running full length both starboard and larboard along her deck-house, where the Gentlemen's and Dining Saloons and most of

185

the staterooms were located, refracted jewel-like the rays of the afternoon sun. Above, to the stern, was the weather deck, on which stretched the texas; this housed luxury state rooms and cabins for the packet's officers. Some distance forward of the texas was the oblong glassed-in structure of the pilothouse.

Smiling as they approached, O'Hara said: "Now ain't she a fine lady?" He spoke with a careless brogue, the result of a strict ethnic upbringing in the Irish Channel section of New Orleans. At times this caused certain individuals to underestimate his capabilities and intelligence, which in his profession was a major asset.

"She *is* fine, Fergus," Hattie agreed. "As fine as any on the Mississippi before the war. How far did you say it was to Stockton?"

O'Hara laughed. "A hundred twenty-seven miles. One night in the lap of luxury is all we'll be having this trip, me lady."

"Pity," Hattie said. She was in her late twenties, five years younger than her husband, dark-complected, buxom. Thick black hair, worn in ringlets, was covered by a lace-decorated bonnet. She wore a gray serge traveling dress, the hem of which was now coated with dust.

O'Hara was tall and plump, and sported a luxuriant red beard of which he was inordinately proud and on which he doted every morning with scissors and comb. Like Hattie, he had mild blue eyes; unlike Hattie, and as a result of a fondness for spirits, he possessed a nose that approximated the color of his beard. He was dressed in a black frock coat, striped trousers, and a flowered vest. He carried no visible weapons, but in a holster inside his coat was a double-action revolver.

The *Delta Star*'s stage plank, set aft to the main deck, was jammed with passengers and wagons; it was not twenty till four. A large group of nankeen-dressed men were congregated near the foot of the plank. All of them wore green felt shamrocks pinned to the lapels of their coats, and several were smoking thin long-nine seegars. Fluttering above them on a pole held by one was a green banner with the words *Mulrooney Guards, San Francisco Company A* crudely printed on it in white.

Four of the group were struggling to lift a massive wooden crate that appeared to be quite heavy. They managed to get it aloft, grunting, and began to stagger with it to the plank. As they started up, two members of the *Delta Star*'s deck crew came down and blocked their way. One of them said: "Before you go any farther, gents, show us your manifest on that box."

One of the other Mulrooneys stepped up the plank. "What manifest?" he demanded. "This ain't cargo, it's personal belongings."

"Anything heavy as that pays cargo," the deckhand said. "Rules is rules and they apply to Bluebellies same as to better folks."

"Bluebellies, is it? Ye damned Copperhead, I'll pound ye up into horsemeat!" And the Mulrooney hit the deckhand on the side of the head and knocked him down.

The second crew member stepped forward and hit the Mulrooney on the side of the head and knocked *him* down.

Another of the guards jumped in and hit the second crewman on the side of the head and knocked *him* down.

The first deckhand got up and the first Mulrooney got up, minus his hat, and began swinging at each other. The second crewman got up and began swinging at the second Mulrooney. The other members of the guards, shouting encouragement, formed a tight circle around the fighting men—all except for the four carrying the heavy wooden crate. Those Mulrooneys struggled up the stage plank with their burden and disappeared among the confusion on the main deck.

The fight did not last long. Several roustabouts and one of the steamer's mates hurried onto the landing and broke it up.

No one seemed to have been injured, save for the two deck-hands who were both unconscious. The mate seemed undecided as to what to do, finally concluded that to do nothing at all was the best recourse; he turned up the plank again. Four roust-abouts carried the limp crewmen up after him, followed by the guards who were all now loudly singing "John Brown's Body".

Hattie asked O'Hara: "Now what was that all about?"

"War business," he told her solemnly. "California's a long way from the battlefields, but feelings and loyalties are as strong here as in the East."

"But who are the Mulrooney Guards?"

Before O'Hara could answer, a tall man wearing a Prince Albert, who was standing next to Hattie, swung toward them and smiled and said: "I couldn't help overhearing the lady's question. If you'll pardon the intrusion, I can supply an answer."

O'Hara looked the tall man over and decided he was a gambler. He had no particular liking for gamblers, but for the most part he was tolerant of them. He said the intrusion was pardoned, introduced himself and Hattie, and learned that the tall man was John A. Colfax, of San Francisco.

Colfax had gray eyes that were both congenial and cunning. In his left hand he continually shuffled half a dozen small bronze war-issue cents—coinage that was not often seen in the West. He said: "The Mulrooney Guards is a more or less official militia company, one of several supporting the Union cause. They have two companies, one in San Francisco and one in Stockton. I imagine this one is joining the other for some sort of celebration."

"Tomorrow is Saint Patrick's Day," O'Hara told him.

"Ah, yes, of course."

"Ye seem to know quite a bit about these lads, Mister Colfax."

"I am a regular passenger on the *Delta Star*," Colfax said.

"On the Sacramento packets as well. A traveling man picks up a good deal of information."

O'Hara said blandly: "Aye, that he does."

Hattie said: "I wonder what the Mulrooneys have in that crate?"

Colfax allowed as how he had no idea. He seemed about to say something further, but the appearance of three closely grouped men, hurrying through the crowd toward the stage plank, claimed his attention. The one in the middle, O'Hara saw, wore a broadcloth suit and a nervous, harried expression, and cradled in both hands against his body was a large and apparently heavy valise. The two men on either side were more roughly dressed, had revolvers holstered at their hips. Their expressions were dispassionate, their eyes watchful.

O'Hara frowned and glanced at Colfax. The gambler watched the trio climb the plank and hurry up the aft stairway, then he said quietly, as if to himself: "It appears we'll be carrying more than passengers and cargo this trip." He regarded the O'Haras again, touched his hat, said it had been a pleasure talking to them, and moved away to board the riverboat.

Hattie looked at her husband inquiringly.

He said: "Gold."

"Gold, Fergus?"

"That nervous chap had the look of a banker, the other two of deputies. A bank transfer of specie or dust from here to Stockton . . . or so I'm thinking."

"Where will they keep it?"

"Purser's office, mayhap. Or the pilothouse."

Hattie and O'Hara climbed the plank. As they were crossing the main deck, the three men appeared again on the stairway; the one in the broadcloth suit looked considerably less nervous now. O'Hara watched them go down onto the landing. Then, shrugging, he followed Hattie up the stairs to the weather deck.

They stopped at the starboard rail to await departure.

Hattie said: "What did you think of Mister Colfax?"

"A slick-tongued lad, even for a gambler. But ye'd not want to be giving him a coin to put in a village poor box for ye."

She laughed. "He seemed rather interested in the delivery of gold, if that's what it was."

"Aye, so he did."

At exactly four o'clock the *Delta Star*'s whistle sounded; her buckets churned the water; steam poured from her twin stacks. She began to move slowly away from the wharf. All up and down the Embarcadero now, whistles sounded and the other packets commenced backing down from their landings. The waters of the bay took on a chaotic appearance as the boats maneuvered for right of way. Clouds of steam filled the sky; the sound of pilot whistles was angry and shrill.

Once the *Delta Star* was clear of the wharves and of other riverboats, her speed increased steadily. Hattie and O'Hara remained at the rail until San Francisco's low, sun-washed skyline had receded into the distance, then they went in search of a steward, who took them to their stateroom. Its windows faced larboard, but its entrance was located inside a tunnel-like hallway down the center of the texas. Spacious and opulent, the cabin contained carved rosewood paneling and red plush upholstery. Hattie said she thought it was grand. O'Hara, who had never been particularly impressed by Victorian elegance, said he imagined she would be wanting to freshen up a bit— and that, so as not to be disturbing her, he would take a stroll about the decks.

"Stay away from the liquor buffet," Hattie said. "The day is young, if I make my meaning clear."

O'Hara sighed. "I had no intention of visiting the liquor buffet," he lied, and sighed again, and left the stateroom.

He wandered aft, past the officers' quarters. When he emerged from the texas, he found himself confronted by the huge A-shaped gallows frame that housed the cylinder, valve gear, beam, and crank of the walking-beam engine. Each stroke of the piston produced a mighty roar and hiss of escaping steam. The noise turned O'Hara around and sent him back through the texas to the forward stairway.

Ahead of him, as he started down, were two men who had come out of the pilothouse. One was tall, with bushy black hair and a thick mustache—apparently a passenger. The second wore a square-billed cap and the sort of stern, authoritative look that would have identified him as the *Delta Star's* pilot even without the cap. At this untroubled point in the journey, the packet would be in the hands of a cub apprentice.

The door to the Gentlemen's Saloon kept intruding on O'Hara's thoughts as he walked about the deckhouse. Finally he went down to the main deck. Here, in the open areas and in the shed-like expanse beneath the superstructures, deck passengers and cargo were pressed together in noisy confusion: men and women and children, wagons and animals and chickens in coops; sacks, bales, boxes, hogsheads, cords of bull pine for the roaring fireboxes under the boilers. And, too, the Mulrooney Guards, who were loosely grouped near the taffrail, alternately singing "The Girl I Left Behind Me" and passing around jugs of what was likely poteen—a powerful homemade Irish whiskey.

O'Hara sauntered near the group, stood with his back against a stanchion, and began to shave cuttings from his tobacco plug into his briar. One of the Mulrooneys—small and fair and feisty-looking—noticed him, studied his luxuriant red beard, and then approached him carrying one of the jugs. Without preamble he demanded to know if the gentleman were Irish. O'Hara said he was, with great dignity. The Mulrooney slapped him on the back. "I knew it!" he said effusively. "Me name's Billy Culligan. Have a drap of the crayture."

O'Hara decided Hattie had told him only to stay away from the buffet. There was no deceit in accepting hospitality from fellows of the Auld Sod. He took the jug, drank deeply, and allowed as how it was a fine crayture, indeed. Then he introduced himself, saying that he and the missus were traveling to Stockton on a business matter.

"Ye won't be conducting business on the morrow, will ye?"

"On Saint Pat's Day?" O'Hara was properly shocked.

"Boyo, I like ye," Culligan said. "How would ye like to join in on the biggest Saint Pat's Day celebration in the entire sovereign state of California?"

"I'd like nothing better."

"Then come to Green Park, on the north of Stockton, 'twixt nine and ten and tell the lads ye're a friend of Billy Culligan. There'll be a parade, and all the food and liquor ye can hold. Oh, it'll be a fine celebration, lad!"

O'Hara said he and the missus would be there, meaning it. Culligan offered another drink of poteen, which O'Hara casually accepted. Then the little Mulrooney stepped forward and said in a conspiratorial voice: "Come 'round here to the taffrail just before we steam into Stockton on the morrow. We've a plan to start off Saint Pat's Day with a mighty salute . . . part of the reason we sent our wives and wee ones ahead on the *San Joaquin*. Ye won't want to be missing that, either." Before O'Hara could ask him what he meant by "mighty salute," he and his jug were gone into the midst of the other guards.

"Me lady," O'Hara said contentedly, "that was a meal fit for royalty and no doubt about it."

Hattie agreed that it had been a sumptuous repast as they walked from the Dining Saloon to the texas stairway. The evening was mild, with little breeze and no sign of the thick tule fog that often made northern California riverboating a hazardous proposition. The *Delta Star*—aglow with hundreds of lights—had come through the Carquinez Straits, passed Chipp's Island, and was now entering the San Joaquin River. A pale moon silvered the water, turned a ghostly white the long stretches of fields along both banks.

On the weather deck, they stood close together at the larboard rail, not far from the pilothouse. For a couple of minutes they were alone. Then footsteps sounded and O'Hara turned to see the ship's captain and pilot returning from their dinner. Touching his cap, the captain—a lean, graying man of fifty-odd—wished them good evening. The pilot merely grunted.

The O'Haras continued to stand looking out at the willows and cottonwoods along the riverbank. Then, suddenly, an explosive, angry cry came from the pilothouse, startling them both. This was followed by muffled voices, another sharp exclamation, movement not clearly perceived through the window glass and beyond partially drawn rear curtains, and several sharp blasts on the pilot whistle.

Natural curiosity drew O'Hara away from the rail, hurrying; Hattie was close behind him. The door to the pilothouse stood open when they reached it, and O'Hara turned inside by one step. The enclosure was almost as opulent as their stateroom, but he noticed its appointments only peripherally. What captured his full attention was three men now grouped before the wheel, and the four items on the floor close to and against the starboard bulkhead.

The pilot stood clutching two of the wheel spokes, red-faced with anger; the captain was bending over the kneeling figure of the third man—a young blond individual wearing a buttoned-up sack coat and baggy trousers, both of which were streaked with dust and soot and grease. The blond lad was making soft moaning sounds, holding the back of his head cupped in one palm.

One of the items on the floor was a steel pry bar. The others were a small safe bolted to the bulkhead, a black valise—the one O'Hara had seen carried by the nervous man and his two bodyguards—and a medium-size iron strongbox, just large enough to have fit inside the valise. The safe door, minus its combination dial, stood wide open; the valise and a strongbox were also open. All three were quite obviously empty.

The pilot jerked the bell knobs, signaling an urgent request to the engineer for a lessening of speed, and began barking stand-by orders into a speaking tube. His was the voice that had startled Hattie and O'Hara. The captain was saying to the blond man: "It's a miracle we didn't drift out of the channel and run afoul of a snag . . . a miracle, Chadwick."

"I can't be held to blame, sir," Chadwick said defensively. "Whoever it was hit me from behind. I was sitting at the wheel when I heard the door open and thought it was you and Mister Bridgeman returning from supper, so I didn't even bother to turn. The next thing, my head seemed to explode. That is all I know."

He managed to regain his feet and moved stiffly to a red plush sofa, hitching up his trousers with one hand; the other still held the back of his head. Bridgeman, the pilot, banged down the speaking tube, then spun the wheel a half turn to larboard. As he did the last, he glanced over his shoulder and saw O'Hara and Hattie. "Get out of here!" he shouted at them. "There is nothing here for you!"

"Perhaps, now, that isn't true," O'Hara said mildly. "Ye've had a robbery, have ye not?"

"That is none of your affair."

Boldly O'Hara came deeper into the pilothouse, motioning Hattie to close the door. She did so. Bridgeman yelled: "I told you to get out of here! Who do you think you are?"

"Fergus O'Hara . . . operative of the Pinkerton Police Agency."

Bridgeman stared at him, open-mouthed. The captain and Chadwick had shifted their attention to him as well. At length, in a less harsh tone, the pilot said: "Pinkerton Agency?"

"Of Chicago, Illinois, Allan Pinkerton, Principal."

O'Hara produced his billfold, extracted from it the letter from Allan Pinkerton and the Chicago & Eastern Central Railroad Pass, both of which identified him, as the bearer of these documents, to be a Pinkerton Police agent. He showed them to both Bridgeman and the captain.

"What would a Pinkerton man be doing 'way out here in California?" the captain asked.

"Me wife Hattie and me are on the trail of a gang that has been terrorizing Adams Express coaches. We've traced them to San Francisco and now have reliable information they're to be found in Stockton."

"Your wife is a Pinkerton agent, too? A woman . . . ?"

O'Hara looked at him as if he might be a dullard. "Ye've never heard of Miss Kate Warne, one of the agency's most trusted Chicago operatives? No, I don't suppose ye have. Well, me wife has no official capacity, but since one of the leaders of this gang is reputed to be a woman, and since Hattie has assisted me in the past, women being able to obtain information in places men cannot, I've brought her along."

Bridgeman said from the wheel: "Well, we can use a trained detective after what has happened here."

O'Hara nodded. "Is it gold ye've had stolen?"

"Gold . . . yes. How did you know that?"

He told them of witnessing the delivery of the valise at Long Wharf. He asked then: "How large an amount is involved?"

"Forty thousand dollars," the captain said.

O'Hara whistled. "That's a fair considerable sum."

"To put it mildly, sir."

"Was it specie or dust?"

"Dust. An urgent consignment from the California Merchant's Bank to their branch in Stockton."

"How many men had foreknowledge of the shipment?"

"The officials of the bank, Mister Bridgeman, and myself."

"No other officers of the packet?"

"No."

"Would you be telling me, Captain, who was present when the delivery was made this afternoon?"

"Mister Bridgeman and I, and a friend of his visiting in San Francisco . . . a newspaperman from Nevada."

O'Hara remembered the tall man with bushy hair who had been with the pilot earlier. "Can ye vouch for this newspaperman?" he asked Bridgeman.

"I can. His reputation is unimpeachable."

"Has anyone other than he been here since the gold was brought aboard?"

"Not to my knowledge."

Chadwick said that no one had come by while he was on duty, and none of them had noticed anyone shirking about at any time. The captain said sourly: "It appears as though almost any man on this packet could be the culprit. Just how do you propose we find out which one, Mister O'Hara?"

O'Hara did not reply. He bent to examine the safe. The combination dial appeared to have been snapped off by a hand with experience at such villainous business. The valise and the strongbox had also been forced. The pry bar was an ordinary tool and had likely also been used as a weapon to knock Chadwick unconscious.

He straightened and moved about the enclosure, studying each fixture. Then he got down on hands and knees and peered under both the sofa and a blackened winter stove. It was under the stove that he found the coin.

His fingers grasped it, closed it into his palm. Standing again, he glanced at the coin and saw that it was made of bronze, a small war-issue cent piece shinily new and free of dust or soot. A smile plucked at the edges of his mouth as he slipped the coin into his vest pocket.

Bridgeman said: "Did you find something?"

"Perhaps. Then again, perhaps not."

O'Hara came forward, paused near where Bridgeman stood at the wheel. Through the windshield he could see the moonlit waters of the San Joaquin. He could also see, as a result of the pilothouse lamps and the darkness without, his own dim reflection in the glass. He thought his stern expression was rather like the one Allan Pinkerton himself possessed.

Bridgeman suggested that crewmen be posted on the lower decks throughout the night, as a precaution in the event the culprit had a confederate with a boat somewhere along the route and intended to leave the packet in the wee hours. The captain thought this was a good idea; so did O'Hara.

He was ready to leave, but the captain had a few more words for him. "I am grateful for your professional assistance, Mister O'Hara, but as master of the *Delta Star* the primary investigative responsibility is mine. Please inform me immediately if you learn anything of significance."

O'Hara said he would.

"Also, I intend my inquiries to be discreet, so as not to alarm the passengers. I'll expect yours to be the same."

"Discretion is me middle name," O'Hara assured him.

A few moments later, he and Hattie were on their way back along the larboard rail to the texas. Hattie, who had been silent during their time in the pilothouse, started to speak, but O'Hara overrode her. "I know what ye're going to say, me lady, and it'll do no good. Me mind's made up. The opportunity to sniff out forty thousand in missing gold is one I'll not pass up."

He left Hattie at the door to their stateroom and hurried to the deckhouse, where he entered the Gentlemen's Saloon. It was a long room, with a liquor buffet at one end and private tables and card layouts spread throughout. A pall of tobacco smoke as thick as tule fog hung in the crowded enclosure.

O'Hara located the shrewd, handsome features of John A. Colfax at a table aft. Two other men were with him: a portly individual with sideburns like miniature tumbleweeds, and the mustached Nevada reporter. They were playing draw poker. O'Hara was not surprised to see that most of the stakes—gold specie and greenbacks—were in front of Colfax.

Casually O'Hara approached the table and stopped behind an empty chair next to the portly man, just as Colfax claimed a pot with four treys. He said: "Good evening, gentlemen."

Colfax greeted him unctuously, asked if he were enjoying the voyage thus far. O'Hara said he was, and observed that the gambler seemed to be enjoying it, too, judging from the stack of legal tender before him. Colfax just smiled. But the portly man said in grumbling tones: "I should damned well say so. He has been taking my money for three solid hours."

"Aye? That long?"

"Since just after dinner."

"Ye've been playing without pause since then?"

"Nearly so," the newspaperman said. Through the tendrils of smoke from his cigar, he studied O'Hara with mild blue eyes. "Why do you ask, sir?"

"Oh, I was thinking I saw Mister Colfax up on the weather deck about an hour ago. Near the pilothouse."

"You must have mistaken someone else for me," Colfax said. Now that the draw game had been momentarily suspended, he had produced a handful of war-issue coins and begun to toy with them as he had done at Long Wharf. "I did leave the table for a few minutes about an hour ago, but only to use the lavatory. I haven't been on the weather deck at all this trip."

O'Hara saw no advantage in pressing the matter. He pretended to notice for the first time the one-cent pieces Colfax was shuffling. "Lucky coins, Mister Colfax?"

"These? Why, yes. I won a sackful of them on a wager once and my luck has been good ever since." Disarming smile. "Gamblers are superstitious about such things, you know."

"Ye don't see many coins like that in California."

"True. They are practically worthless out here."

"So worthless," the reporter said, "that I have seen them used to decorate various leather goods."

The portly man said irritably: "To hell with lucky coins and such nonsense. Are we going to play poker or have a gabfest?"

"Poker, by all means," Colfax said. He slipped the war-issue cents into a pocket of his Prince Albert and reached for the cards. His interest in O'Hara seemed to have vanished.

The reporter, however, was still looking at him with curiosity. "Perhaps you'd care to join us?"

O'Hara declined, saying he had never had any luck with the pasteboards. Then he left the saloon and went in search of the *Delta Star*'s purser. It took him ten minutes to find the man, and thirty seconds to learn that John A. Colfax did not have a stateroom either in the texas or on the deckhouse. The purser, who knew Colfax as a regular passenger, said wryly that the gambler would spend the entire voyage in the Gentlemen's Saloon, having gullible citizens for a ride.

O'Hara returned to the saloon, this time to avail himself of the liquor buffet. He ordered a shot of rye from a bartender who owned a resplendent handlebar moustache, and tossed it down without his customary enjoyment. Immediately he ordered another.

Colfax might well be his man; there was the war-issue coin he'd found under the pilothouse stove, and the fact that Colfax had left the poker game at about the time of the robbery. And yet—what could he have done with the gold? The weight of $40,000 in dust was considerable; he could not very well carry it in his pockets. He had been gone from the poker game long enough to commit the robbery, perhaps, but hardly long enough to have also hidden the spoils.

There were other factors weighing against Colfax, too. One: gentlemen gamblers made considerable sums of money at their trade; they seldom found it necessary to resort to baser thievery. Two: how could Colfax, while sitting here in the saloon, have known when only one man would be present in the pilothouse? An accomplice might have been on watch—but, if there were such a second party, why hadn't he committed the robbery himself?

O'Hara scowled, put away his second rye. If Colfax wasn't the culprit, then who was? And what was the significance of the coin he had found in the pilothouse?

Perhaps the coin had no significance at all, but his instincts told him it did, and he had always trusted his instincts. If not to Colfax, then to whom did it point? Answer: to no one, and to everyone. Even though war-issue cents were uncommon in California, at least half a dozen men presently on board might have one or two in their pockets.

A remark passed by the newspaperman came back to him: such coins were used to decorate various leather goods. Aye, that was a possibility. If the guilty man had been wearing a holster or vest or some other article adorned with the cent pieces, one might have popped loose unnoticed.

O'Hara slid the coin from his pocket and examined it carefully. There were small scratches on its surface that might have been made by stud fasteners, but he couldn't be sure. The scratches might also have been caused by any one of a hundred other means—and the coin could still belong to John A. Colfax.

Returning it to his vest pocket, O'Hara considered the idea of conducting a search for a man wearing leather ornamented with bronze war coins. And dismissed it immediately as folly. He could roam the *Delta Star* all night and not encounter even two-thirds of the passengers. Or he might find someone wearing such an article who would turn out to be completely innocent. And what if the robber had discovered the loss of the coin and chucked the article overboard?

Frustration began to assail him now. But it did not dull his determination. If any man aboard the *Delta Star* could fetch up both the thief and the gold before the packet reached Stockton, that man was Fergus O'Hara, and by damn, if such were humanly possible, he meant to do it!

He left the saloon again and went up to the pilothouse. Bridgeman was alone at the wheel. "What news, O'Hara?" he asked.

"None as yet. Would ye know where the captain is?"

Bridgeman shook his head. "Young fool Chadwick was feeling dizzy from that blow on the head. The captain took him to his quarters just after you and your wife left, and then went to make his inquiries. I expect he's still making 'em."

O'Hara sat on the red plush sofa, packed and lighted his pipe, and let his mind drift along various channels. After a time something in his memory flickered like a guttering candle—and then died before he could steady the flame. When he was unable to rekindle the flame, he roared forth with a venomous ten-jointed oath that startled even Bridgeman.

Presently the captain returned to the pilothouse. He and O'Hara exchanged identical expectant looks, which immediately told each that the other had uncovered nothing of significance. Verbal confirmation of this was brief, after which the captain said bleakly: "The prospects are grim, Mister O'Hara. Grim, indeed."

"We've not yet come into Stockton," O'Hara reminded him.

The captain sighed. "We have no idea of who is guilty, thus no idea of where to find the gold . . . if in fact it is still on board. We haven't the manpower for a search of packet and passengers before our arrival. And afterward . . . I don't see how we can hope to hold everyone on board while the authorities are summoned and a search mounted. Miners are a hot-headed lot. So are those Irish militiamen. We would likely have a riot on our hands."

O'Hara had nothing more to say. By all the saints, he was not yet ready to admit defeat. He bid the captain and Bridgeman good night, and spent the next hour prowling the decks and cudgeling his brain. It seemed to him that he had seen and heard enough since the robbery to know who it was he was after and where the missing gold could be found. If only he could bring forth one scrap of this knowledge from his memory, he was certain the others would follow. . . .

Maddeningly, however, no scrap was forthcoming. Not while he prowled the decks, not after he returned to his stateroom— Hattie, he was relieved to find, was already fast asleep—and not when the first light of dawn crept into the sky beyond the window.

When the *Delta Star* came out of one of the snake-like bends in the river and started down the last long reach to Stockton, O'Hara was standing with Hattie at the starboard deckhouse rail. It was just past 7:30—a spring-crisp, cloudless St. Patrick's Day morning—and the steamer would dock in another thirty minutes.

O'Hara was in a foul humor: three-quarters frustration and one-quarter lack of sleep. He had left the stateroom at six o'clock and gone up to the pilothouse and found the captain, Bridgeman, and Chadwick drinking coffee thickened with molasses. They had nothing to tell him. And their humors had been no better than his; it seemed that as a result of O'Hara's failure to perform as advertised, he had fallen out of favor with them.

Staring down at the slow-moving waters frothed by the side-wheel, he told himself for the thousandth time: *Ye've got the answer, ye know ye do. Think, lad! Dredge it up before it's too late. . . .*

A voice beside him said: "Fine morning, isn't it?"

Irritably O'Hara turned his head and found himself looking into the cheerfully smiling visage of the Nevada newspaperman. The bushy-haired lad's eyes were red-veined from a long night in the Gentlemen's Saloon, but this did not seem to have had any effect on his disposition.

O'Hara grunted. "Is it?" he said grumpily. "Ye sound as if ye have cause for rejoicing. Did ye win a hatful of specie from the gambler Colfax last night?"

"Unfortunately, no. I lost a fair sum, as a matter of fact. Gambling is one of my sadder vices, along with a fondness for the social drink. But then, a man may have no bad habits and have worse."

O'Hara grunted again and looked out over the broad, yellow-ish land of the San Joaquin Valley.

The reporter's gaze was on the river. "Clear as a mirror, isn't it?" he said nostalgically. "Not at all like the Mississippi. I remember when I was a boy. . . ."

O'Hara had jerked upright, into a posture as rigid as an obelisk. He stood that way for several seconds. Then he said explosively: "In the name of Patrick and all the saints!"

Hattie said with alarm in her voice: "Fergus, what is it?"

O'Hara grinned at her, swung around to the newspaperman, and clapped him exuberantly on the shoulder. "Lad, it may yet be a fine a morning. It may yet be, indeed."

He told Hattie to wait there for him, left her and the bewildered reporter at the rail, and hurried down to the aft stairway. On the weather deck, he moved aft of the texas and stopped before the gallows frame.

There was no one in the immediate vicinity. O'Hara stepped up close to the frame and eased his head and both arms inside the vent opening, avoiding the machinery of the massive walking-beam. Heat and the heavy odor of cylinder oil assailed him; the throb of the piston was almost deafening.

With his left hand he felt along the interior wall of the frame, his fingertips encountering a greasy build-up of oil and dust. It was only a few seconds before they located a metal hook screwed into the wood. A new hook, free of grease; he was able to determine that by touching it with the clean fingers of his right hand. Nothing was suspended from the hook, but O'Hara was now certain that something had been during most of the night.

He was also certain that he knew where it could be found at this very moment.

When he withdrew his head and arms from the vent opening, grease stained his hands and his coat and shirt sleeves, and he was sweating from the heat. He used his handkerchief, then hastened across to enter the texas. There were identifying plates screwed to the doors of the officers' cabins; he stopped before the one he wanted, drew his coat away from his revolver, and laid the fingers of his right hand on its grip. With his left hand he rapped on the door panel.

There was no response.

He knocked again, waited, then took out his pocket knife. The door latch yielded in short order to rapid manipulations with one of the blades. He slipped inside and shut the door behind him.

A brief look around convinced him that the most likely hiding place was a dark corner formed by the single bunk bed and an open-topped wooden tool carrier. And that in fact was where he found what he was looking for: a wide leather belt ornamented with bronze war-issue coins, and a greasy calf-skin grip. He drew the bag out, worked at the locked catch with his knife, and got it open.

The missing gold was inside, in two score small pouches.

O'Hara looked at the sacks for several seconds, smiling. Then he found himself thinking of the captain, and of the bank in Stockton that urgently awaited the consignment. He sobered, shook himself mentally. This was neither the time nor the place for rumination; there was still much to be done. He refastened the grip, hefted it, and started to rise.

Scraping noise on the deck outside. Then the cabin door burst open, and the man whose quarters these were, the man who had stolen the gold, stood framed in the opening.

Chadwick, the cub pilot.

Recognition darkened his face with the blood of rage. He growled: "So you found out, did you? You damned Pinkerton meddler!" And he launched himself across the cabin.

O'Hara moved to draw his revolver too late. By then Chadwick was on him. The young pilot's shoulder struck the carpetbag that O'Hara thrust up defensively, sandwiched it between them as they went crashing into the larboard bulkhead. The impact broke them apart. O'Hara spilled sideways across the bunk, with the grip between his legs, and cracked his head on the rounded projection of wood that served as headboard. An eruption of pain blurred his vision, kept him from reacting as quickly as he might have. Chadwick was on him again before he could disengage himself from the bag.

A wild blow grazed the side of O'Hara's head. He threw up a forearm, succeeded in warding off a second blow, but not a third. That one connected solidly with his jaw, and his vision went cock-eyed again.

He was still conscious, but he seemed to have momentarily lost all power of movement. The flailing weight that was Chadwick lifted from him. There were scuffling sounds, then the sharp running slap of boots receding across the cabin and on the deck outside.

O'Hara's jaw and the back of his head began a simultaneous and painful throbbing; at the same time strength seemed to flow back into his arms and legs. Shaking his head to clear his vision, he swung off the bunk and let loose with a many-jointed oath that even his grandfather, who had always sworn he could out-cuss Old Nick himself, would have been proud to call his own. When he could see again, he realized that Chadwick had caught up the calf-skin grip and taken it with him. He hobbled to the door and turned to larboard out of it, the way the running steps had gone.

Chadwick, hampered by the weight and bulk of the grip, was at the bottom of the aft stairway when O'Hara reached the top. He glanced upward, saw O'Hara, and began to race frantically toward the nearby main deck staircase. He banged into passengers, scattering them, whirled a fat woman around like a ballerina executing a pirouette, and sent the reticule she had been carrying over the rail into the river.

Men commenced calling in angry voices and milling about as O'Hara tumbled down the stairs to the deckhouse. A bearded, red-shirted miner stepped into Chadwick's path at the top of the main deck stairway; without slowing, the cub pilot bowled him over as if he were a giant ninepin and went down the stairs in a headlong dash. O'Hara lurched through the confusion of passengers and descended after him, cursing eloquently all the while.

Chadwick shoved two startled Chinese out of the way at the foot of the stairs and raced toward the taffrail, looking back over his shoulder. The bloody fool was going to jump into the river, O'Hara thought. And when he did, the weight of the gold would take both him and the bag straight to the bottom. . . .

All at once O'Hara became aware that there were not many passengers inhabiting the aft section of the main deck, when there should have been a clotted mass of them. Some of those who were present had heard the commotion on the upper deck and been drawn to the staircase; the rest were split into two groups, one lining the larboard rail and the other lining the starboard, and their attention was held by a different spectacle. Some were murmuring excitedly; others looked amused; still others wore apprehensive expressions. The center section of the deck opposite the taffrail was completely cleared.

The reason for this was that a small, rusted, and very old half-pounder had been set up on wooden chocks at the taffrail, aimed downriver like an impolitely pointing finger.

Beside the cannon was a keg of black powder and a charred-looking ramrod.

And surrounding the cannon were the Mulrooney Guards, one of whom held a firebrand poised above the fuse vent and all of whom were now loudly singing "The Wearing of the Green".

O'Hara knew in that moment what it was the Mulrooneys had had secreted inside their wooden crate, and why they had been so anxious to get it aboard without having the contents examined, and he knew the meaning of Billy Culligan's remark about planning to start off St. Patrick's day with a mighty salute. He stopped running and opened his mouth to shout at Chadwick, who was still fleeing and still looking back over his shoulder. He could not recall afterward if he actually did shout or not; if so, it was akin to whispering in a thunderstorm.

The Mulrooney cannoneer touched off the fuse. The other Mulrooney Guards scattered, still singing. The watching passengers huddled farther back, some averting their eyes. Chadwick kept on running toward the taffrail.

And the cannon, as well as the keg of black powder, promptly blew up.

The *Delta Star* lurched and rolled with the sudden concussion. A great sweeping cloud of sulphurous black smoke enveloped the riverboat. O'Hara caught hold of one of the uprights in the starboard rail and clung to it, coughing and choking. *Too much black powder and not enough bracing,* he thought. Then he thought: *I hope Hattie had the good sense to stay where she was on the deckhouse.*

The steamer was in a state of bedlam, everyone on each of the three decks screaming or shouting. Some of the passengers thought a boiler had exploded, a common steamboat hazard. When the smoke finally began to dissipate, O'Hara looked in the direction of the center taffrail and discovered that most of it, like the cannon, was missing. The deck in that area was blackened and scarred, some of the boarding torn into splinters.

But there did not seem to have been any casualties. A few passengers had received minor injuries, most of them Mulrooney Guards, and several were speckled with black soot. No one had fallen overboard. Even Chadwick had miraculously managed to survive the concussion, despite his proximity to the cannon when it and the powder keg had gone up. He was moaning feebly and moving his arms and legs, looking like a bedraggled chimney sweep, when O'Hara reached his side.

The grip containing the gold had fared somewhat better. Chadwick had been shielding it with his body at the moment of the blast, and, while it was torn open and the leather pouches scattered about, most of the sacks were intact. One or two had split open, and particles of gold dust glittered in the sooty air. The preponderance of passengers were too concerned with their own welfare to notice; those who did stared with disbelief but kept their distance, for no sooner had O'Hara reached Chadwick than the captain and half a dozen of the deck crew arrived.

"Chadwick?" the captain said in amazement. "Chadwick's the thief?"

"Aye, he's the one."

"But . . . what happened? What was he doing here with the gold?"

"I was chasing him, the spalpeen."

"You were? Then . . . you knew of his guilt before the explosion? How?"

"I'll explain it all to ye later," O'Hara said. "Right now there's me wife to consider."

He left the bewildered captain and his crew to attend to Chadwick and the gold, and went to find Hattie.

Shortly past 9:00, an hour after the *Delta Star* had docked at the foot of Stockton's Center Street, O'Hara stood with Hattie and a group of men on the landing. He wore his last clean suit, a broadcloth, and a bright green tie in honor of St. Patrick's Day. The others, clustered around him, were Bridgeman, the captain, the Nevada reporter, a hawkish man who was Stockton's sheriff, and two officials of the California Merchants Bank. Chadwick had been removed to the local jail in the company of a pair of deputies and a doctor. The Mulrooney Guards, after medical treatment, a severe reprimand, and a promise to pay all damages to the packet, had been released to continue their merry-making in Green Park.

The captain was saying: "We are all deeply indebted to you, Mister O'Hara. It would have been a black day if Chadwick had succeeded in escaping with the gold . . . a black day for us all."

"I only did me duty," O'Hara said solemnly.

"It is unfortunate that the California Merchants Bank cannot offer you a reward," one of the bank officials said. "However, we

are not a wealthy concern, as our urgent need for the consignment of dust attests. But I don't suppose you could accept a
reward in any case . . . the Pinkertons never do, I'm told."

"Aye, that's true."

Bridgeman said: "Will you explain now how you knew Chadwick was the culprit? And how he accomplished the theft? He
refused to confess, you know."

O'Hara nodded. He told them of finding the war-issue coin
under the pilothouse stove; his early suspicions of the gambler,
Colfax; the reporter's remark that such coins were being used
in California to decorate leather goods; his growing certainty
that he had seen and heard enough to piece together the truth,
and yet his maddening inability to cudgel forth the necessary
scraps from his memory.

"It wasn't until this morning that the doors in me mind finally
opened," he said. He looked at the newspaperman. "It was this
gentleman that gave me the key."

The reporter was surprised. "I gave you the key?"

"Ye did," O'Hara told him. "Ye said of the river . . . clear as a
mirror, isn't it? Do ye remember saying that, while we were
together at the rail?"

"I do. But I don't see. . . ."

"It was the word mirror," O'Hara said. "It caused me to
think of reflection, and all at once I was recalling how I'd been
able to see me own image in the pilothouse windshield soon
after the robbery. Yet Chadwick claimed he was sitting in the
pilot's seat when he heard the door open just before he was
struck, and that he didn't turn because he thought it was the
captain and Mister Bridgeman returning from supper. But if I
was able to see me reflection in the glass, Chadwick would sure
have been able to see his . . . and anybody creeping up behind
him.

"Then I recalled something else. Chadwick had his coat buttoned when I first entered the pilothouse, on a warm night like the last. Why? And why did his trousers look so baggy, as though they might fall down? Well, then, the answer was this. After Chadwick broke open the safe and the strongbox, his problem was what to do with the gold. He couldn't risk a trip to his quarters while he was alone in the pilothouse. He might be seen, and there was also the possibility that the *Delta Star* would run into a bar or snag if she slipped off course. D'ye recall saying it was a miracle such hadn't happened, Captain, thinking as ye were then that Chadwick had been unconscious for some time?"

The captain said he did.

"So Chadwick had to have the gold on his person," O'Hara said, "when you and Mister Bridgeman found him, and when Hattie and I entered soon afterward. He couldn't have removed it until later, when he claimed to be feeling dizzy and you escorted him to his cabin. That, now, is the significance of the buttoned coat and the baggy trousers. What he must have done was to take off his belt, the wide one decorated with war-issue coins that I found in his cabin, and use it to strap the gold pouches above his waist . . . a makeshift money belt, ye see. He was in such a rush, for fear of being found out, that he failed to notice when one of the coins popped loose and rolled under the stove.

"Once he had the pouches secured, he waited until he heard Mister Bridgeman and the captain returning, the while tending to his piloting duties. Then he lay down on the floor and pretended to've been knocked senseless. He kept his loose coat buttoned for fear someone would notice the thickness about his upper middle, and that he was no longer wearing his belt in its proper place, and he kept hitching up his trousers because he *wasn't* wearing the belt in its proper place."

Hattie took her husband's arm. "Fergus, what did Chadwick

do with the gold afterward? Did he have it hidden in his quarters all along?"

"No, me lady. I expect he was afraid of a search, so first chance he had he put the gold into the calf-skin grip, and then hung the grip from a metal hook inside the gallows frame."

The Stockton sheriff asked: "How could you possibly have deduced that fact?"

"While in the pilothouse after the robbery," O'Hara said, "I noticed that Chadwick's coat was soiled with dust and soot from his lying on the floor. But it also showed streaks of grease, which couldn't have come from the floor. When the other pieces fell into place this morning, I reasoned that he might have picked up the grease marks while making preparations to hide the gold. My consideration then was that he'd have wanted a place close to his quarters, and the only such place with grease about it was the gallows frame. The hook I discovered inside was new and free of grease. Chadwick, therefore, must have put it there only recently . . . tonight, in fact, thus accounting for the grease on his coat."

"Amazing detective work," the reporter said, "simply amazing."

Everyone else agreed.

"You really are a fine detective, Fergus O'Hara," Hattie said. "Amazing, indeed."

O'Hara said nothing. Now that they were five minutes parted from the others, walking alone together along Stockton's dusty main street, he had begun scowling and grumbling to himself.

Hattie ventured: "It's a splendid, sunny Saint Patrick's Day. Shall we join the festivities in Green Park?"

"We've nothing to celebrate," O'Hara muttered.

"Still thinking about the gold, are you?"

"And what else would I be thinking about?" he said. "Fine

detective . . . faugh! Some consolation that is!"

It was Hattie's turn to be silent.

O'Hara wondered sourly what those lads back at the landing would say if they knew the truth of the matter—that he was no more a Pinkerton operative than were the Mulrooney Guards. That he had only been impersonating one toward his own ends, in this case and others since he had taken the railroad pass and letter of introduction off the chap in St. Louis the previous year—the Pinkerton chap who'd foolishly believed he was taking O'Hara to jail. That he had wanted the missing pouches of gold for himself and Hattie. And that he, Fergus O'Hara, was the finest confidence man in these sovereign United States, come to Stockton, California to have for a ride a banker who intended to cheat the government by buying up Indian land.

Well, those lads would never know any of this, because he had duped them all—brilliantly, as always. And for nothing. Nothing!

He moaned aloud: "Forty thousand in gold, Hattie. Forty thousand that I was holding in me hands, clutched fair to me black heart, when that rascal Chadwick burst in on me. Two more minutes, just two more minutes. . . ."

"It was Providence," she said. "You were never meant to have that gold, Fergus."

"What d'ye mean? The field was white for the sickle. . . ."

"Not a bit of that," Hattie said. "And if you'll be truthful with yourself, you'll admit you enjoyed every minute of your play-acting of a detective . . . every minute of the explaining just now of your brilliant deductions."

"I didn't," O'Hara lied weakly. "I hate detectives. . . ."

"*Bosh.* I'm glad the gold went to its rightful owners, and you should be, too, because your heart is about as black as this sunny morning. You've only stolen from dishonest men in all the time I've known you. Why, if you had succeeded in filching the gold, you'd have begun despising yourself sooner than you realize . . . not only because it belongs to honest citizens, but because you would have committed the crime on Saint Patrick's Day. If you stop to consider it, you wouldn't commit any crime on Saint Pat's Day, now, would you?"

O'Hara grumbled and glowered, but he was remembering his thoughts in Chadwick's cabin, when he had held the gold in his hands—thoughts of the captain's reputation and possible loss of position, and of the urgent need of the new branch bank in Stockton. He was not at all sure, now, that he would have kept the pouches if Chadwick had not burst in on him. He might well have returned them to the captain. Confound it, that was just what he would have done.

Hattie was right about St. Pat's Day, too. He would not feel decent if he committed a crime on. . . .

Abruptly he stopped walking. Then he put down their luggage and said: "You wait here, me lady. There's something that needs doing before we set off for Green Park."

Before Hattie could speak, he was on his way through clattering wagons and carriages to where a tow-headed boy was scuffling with a mongrel dog. He halted before the boy. "Now then, lad, how would ye like to have a dollar for twenty minutes' good work?"

The boy's eyes grew wide. "What do I have to do, mister?"

O'Hara removed from the inside pocket of his coat an expensive gold American Horologe watch, which happened to be in his possession as the result of a momentary lapse in good sense and fingers made nimble during his misspent youth in New Orleans. He extended it to the boy.

"Take this down to the *Delta Star* steamboat and look about for a tall gentleman with a mustache and a fine head of bushy hair, a newspaperman from Nevada. When ye've found him, give him the watch and tell him Mister Fergus O'Hara came upon it, is returning it, and wishes him a happy Saint Patrick's Day."

"What's his name, mister?" the boy asked. "It'll help me find him quicker."

O'Hara could not seem to recall it, if he had ever heard it in the first place. He took the watch again, opened the hunting-style case, and saw that a name had been etched in flowing script on the dust cover. He handed the watch back to the boy.

"Clemens, it is," O'Hara said then. "A Mister Samuel Langhorne Clemens. . . ."

ADDITIONAL COPYRIGHT INFORMATION

ABOUT THE AUTHOR

Bill Pronzini was born in Petaluma, California. His earliest Western fiction was the short story, "Sawtooth Justice", published in *Zane Grey Western Magazine* (11/69). A number of short stories followed before he published his first Western novel, *The Gallows Land* (1983). Although Pronzini has earned an enviable reputation as an author of detective stories, he has continued periodically to write Western novels, most notably perhaps *Starvation Camp* (1984) and *Firewind* (1989) as well as Western short stories, including *Burgade's Crossing* (Five Star Westerns, 2003) and Quincannon's Game (Five Star Westerns, 2005), both collections of Quincannon stories. In his Western stories, Pronzini has tended toward narratives that avoid excessive violence and, instead, are character studies in which a person has to deal with personal flaws or learn to live with the consequences of previous actions. As an editor and anthologist, Pronzini has demonstrated both rare *éclat* and reliable good taste in selecting very fine stories by other authors, fiction notable for its human drama and memorable characters. He is married to author Marcia Muller, who has written Western stories as well as detective stories, and occasionally collaborated with her husband on detective novels. They make their home in Petaluma, California. *Crucifixion River* with Marcia Muller will be his next Five Star Western.